Beautiful

The look on his face when she came downstairs warmed her from head to toe.

"You look beautiful," he said softly, handing her a large white box and an even larger smile.

"Thank you. So do you." And he did.

"Ready?" he asked when the corsage was fastened securely.

"Ready." She smiled. Hadn't she been ready for this all her life?

They left for the ball.

**Other Point paperbacks
you will want to read:**

Slow Dance

Diane Hoh

SCHOLASTIC INC.
New York Toronto London Auckland Sydney

ISBN 0-590-42387-8

12 11 10 9 8 7 6 5 4 3 2 1   9/8 0 1 2 3 4/9

Printed in the U.S.A.   01

First Scholastic printing, July 1989

Chapter 1

Lauren Tolliver, her long, lean body clad in a royal blue one-piece bathing suit, stood poised at the edge of a diving board. From that vantage point high above the pool's silvery-blue water, she could see most of Drifting Dunes Beach and Tennis Club. Half a dozen tennis courts lay off to her right. The sounds of early August tournaments, *ka-thunk* and *thwoop*, rang in the air. To her left, through tall clumps of red oleander, lay the path to the steep stairs leading down to the beach and the ocean. Straight ahead in the distance, beyond the pool, the Drifting Dunes golf course stretched across rolling green knolls, brown sand traps, and small ponds of brackish green water. Lauren could see tiny little figures sauntering after their little pockmarked white balls.

Behind her, the clubhouse sat high on a green, velvety ridge, its gray shingles turned a pale silver by the salty wind from the sea. Long, narrow windows overlooked the beach below, and wide wooden decks provided astonishing views of the ocean and the sunsets for guests at what was commonly known as simply "The Dunes."

Below her, the pool, the largest in the small coastal town of Oceanview, waited for her. Its blue tiled edges were crowded with escapees from August's heavy mugginess. Sitting, standing, lounging in lawn chairs and at tables, people who found the ocean too turbulent, too awesome, gathered around the pool.

Lauren was not awed by the ocean. She loved the ocean. She had chosen the pool today for one reason only. She chose it because Rick Leon chose it. The Dunes grapevine, usually reliable, had it that Rick had recently detached himself from Sue Browning, his longtime girlfriend. It occurred to Lauren that a perfectly stunning, awe-inspiring half gainer from the high diving board just might yank Rick's attention away from that styrofoam cup he seemed so fascinated with. It was worth a try.

So, thick, dark hair tied up in a curly ponytail, Lauren climbed the ladder, walked the length of the board, edged up on her toes, stretched out her tanned arms, and concentrated. Perfect timing, that was the important thing. Ignore the splashing and shouting, the laughing and chattering going on below, and concentrate. She closed her eyes.

Behind her, two little boys in red swimming trunks raced up the metal ladder, laughing. They had been told more than once to follow the pool rules at The Dunes: no running, no spitting, and always, *always* wait in turn at the diving board. Sometimes they actually followed those rules. This was not one of those times.

Caught up in their giggling race, they either chose to ignore, or failed to see, Lauren. She certainly failed to see them, probably because she was so busy concentrating. Not that noticing the racing boys headed straight for her would have helped. She could hardly have stepped aside to let them pass. Where is there to go on a diving board but off it?

And off it she went, propelled in this instance by the bodies of two healthy, chunky young boys who hit her with full force. Lauren's lovely dive, meant to impress Rick Leon, became a shocked, gasping tumble of long legs and arms flailing in the air.

She was followed closely by her two assailants, and as all three hit the water, a knee cracked Lauren sharply on the side of her head. She sank like a stone.

The next thing she knew, she was clutching the side of the pool, gasping for breath, and being supported by very capable hands. She turned her head to see who belonged to the hands.

He was cute. Very cute. Thick brown hair, wet now, one lock falling across warm, brown, cocker spaniel eyes. Strong, square face. Crooked grin.

"You okay?" he asked.

She nodded, flushing at the thought of how foolish she must have looked, tumbling off the board that way. Like the Scarecrow in *The Wizard of Oz* — no bones, no muscle, just straw and hay in her arms and legs. And she was such a *good* diver, when she wasn't being ambushed.

She took several deep, steadying breaths before answering, "I'm okay enough to strangle the little beasts who ran into me!"

"They're my brothers," the very cute boy said.

Lauren closed her mouth.

"I'm sorry," he added.

"You're sorry they're your brothers? Well, I can certainly understand that."

He laughed. "Well, that, too. But I meant, I'm sorry they sneaked up on you like that. You could have really been hurt. You weren't, were you?"

"Just my pride." She tilted her head a little, hoping she could catch sight of Rick Leon. Was he watching? Maybe she'd been really lucky and he'd missed the laughable dive but was catching the second act: Lauren Tolliver passing the time with a cute male person. Maybe that would catch his eye. Of course, if the dive had caught his eye first, there was no hope.

"It's amazing that you let those two run around loose like that," Lauren said. "Have you or your parents ever seriously considered captivity? As in cages?"

Another laugh. It was a nice laugh. Not too shrill, not too loud, not harsh or silly. Just a nice laugh. "They're twins," he volunteered, "and spoiled rotten. They've been banished to the showers. No swimming for the rest of the week."

"Is this how you spend your summers," she asked, "rescuing your brothers' victims?"

His laugh was the sort of sound you could listen to a lot, given the choice. "No. They usually go away to camp. My folks couldn't afford it this summer, so the demons have been among us since June."

She shook her head. "And you've survived. Amazing!" It was hard to believe that someone with a membership at The Dunes couldn't afford something. Maybe he came here on a day pass. A lot of people from town did. They weren't members, either.

Seeing the look on her face, he explained, "We're not really members here. My dad's managing the Golf Shop this summer, so we have privileges here. The rest of the year he teaches. High school. Trig."

Lauren shuddered.

"Yeah, me, too," he said, nodding.

"I'm not really a member, either," she said. "My grandmother gave me a summer membership for my birthday." She grinned, brushing one dark, damp curl away from her forehead. "She's rich. We're not."

"That sounds intriguing. Why don't we climb out of this very crowded pool and you can tell me all about your rich grandmother? I'll even foot the bill for a couple of cold drinks."

Lauren smiled. "Great. Your brothers won't be joining us, will they?"

He hoisted himself up over the edge of the pool and knelt to lend her a hand. "If they do, we'll toss them into the deep end of the pool."

Lauren shook her head. "We can't," she reminded him as he helped her out of the water. "You gave them an order, remember? No more swimming for the rest of the week."

Lauren was laughing as she stood up and faced her rescuer. The laughter stopped abruptly. Her heart sank just as her body had moments before. Because while he was still cute and nice and funny, he was also . . . a full four inches shorter than her. They were both in their bare feet, but she knew shoes wouldn't help. Unless his were elevator shoes or high heels.

As if he hadn't noticed the difference in their height, he extended a hand. "I'm Neal Winthrop."

Lost in disappointment, Lauren said, "Hi. Lauren Short." She gasped in horror. "Um . . . I mean, Lauren Tolliver." Stupid, stupid girl! He'd *hate* her now. If there was anything worse than being a fifteen-year-old girl whose five feet, nine inches were constantly being pointed out to her, it was probably being a short boy. Unless you were Michael J. Fox. And now that she thought about it, this boy who now hated her was every bit as cute as the actor.

Neal completely ignored her blunder, simply saying, "C'mon, let's go find a table with an umbrella stuck in the middle of it. I've had enough of Old Sol for today. And I'll go get those cold drinks I promised."

Lauren heaved a sigh of relief. He was the forgiving type. Great! Because this was not the sort of person whose feelings she wanted to hurt.

They walked along the tiles to a table, accompanied by calls of, "Hey, Neal, how's it goin'?" and

"Hi, Neal, want to sit here?" But Neal declined with a polite smile and led Lauren to a table at one end of the pool, far enough from the water to avoid being splashed.

"You must know everyone here," she said. "Were you here last summer, too?"

He shook his head. "Nope." He grinned. "I guess they're all hoping for a discount at the Golf Shop. Look, don't go away. I'll be right back."

Lauren watched him go. He walked confidently, smiling and waving at people sitting around tables and lounging by the pool. No wonder she'd never noticed him before. He had probably always been in the middle of a large crowd. And small wonder. He really was nice.

Get a grip on yourself, Lauren, she scolded mentally. The is *not* why you're at The Dunes.

She sat alone at the round, white aluminum table, toying with the fringe on the blue-and-white-checked tablecloth, and thought about why she *was* there.

Lauren Marie Tolliver didn't ask that much from life. Most of what she wanted, she already had: a family that didn't drive her totally mad, a roof with no holes over her head, enough money to buy mascara and records, and a small, hairy dog named Josh who curled up at the foot of her bed every night, making her feel safe. She had plenty of friends, enough intelligence to keep her from making an idiot of herself, and she wasn't ugly. Small children didn't bury their faces in their mothers' laps when Lauren passed by. In fact, small children usually smiled at her. But maybe, Lauren thought, that's because I remind them of the beanstalk in the fairy tale.

For all of those good things in her life, Lauren was grateful.

But what she really wanted, more than anything, was to be . . . four inches shorter. That didn't seem unreasonable to her. If they could put men on the moon and invent pantyhose, surely they could figure out a way to lop a mere four inches off a five-foot, nine-inch female living in a world of short males. Later on, when she was living in a world of grown-up men whose growth hormones finally caught up with them, she could have the four inches put back on.

It was really hard being a tall fifteen-year-old girl. She'd heard every tall joke in the entire world. And she'd reached the point where if one more shrimp of a boy called out to her, "Hey, how's the weather up there?" or, "Are all the creatures on your planet that tall?" she was going to bend down and smack the Lilliputian, sending him flying like tumbleweed.

How *is* it up here? It's lonely!

So, when Lauren's grandmother presented her with a summer membership to The Dunes, Lauren thought, Maybe rich boys are taller. Maybe rich people give their sons fancy European vitamins, from those fancy clinics in Switzerland where they do weird things with sheep glands. And then maybe the boys shoot straight up to the sky like rockets.

It wasn't that she wanted a rich boy. She didn't care about that. She just wanted a *tall* boy. Someone she could look up to — literally.

But even if she didn't meet anyone near her height, Drifting Dunes was a wonderful place to be on a hot summer day. Mornings she helped her father out at his veterinary clinic in town, but that left her afternoons free. Hot and free. What better way to cool off than in the wild and salty ocean or the fresh, cool water of The Dunes' beautiful pool?

And then there was the Sandcastles Ball, the biggest dance of the season, held on Labor Day weekend as a farewell to summer. What would it be like to dance with someone whose head wasn't level with her chest? Wouldn't it be sheer heaven? It *could* happen. People came to the club from all over, not just from Oceanview. If all of the tall boys at her school were already taken, maybe there were boys from other towns who were still unattached.

So, Lauren asked herself, why am I sitting here at this table waiting for someone who just doesn't measure up?

"Hi, you lucky dog!"

Lauren looked up to see Cecelia Burke standing in front of her. Thin and blonde (and incredibly petite), in a brief red bikini, "Silly" was grinning at Lauren.

"I resent being called a canine," Lauren said mildly, "but I wish you'd fill me in on why I'm so lucky."

Silly yanked her bikini top upward and looked at Lauren with round blue eyes. "Are you kidding? Did I or did I not see Neal Winthrop seat you in this very spot?"

Lauren grinned. The rich seated each other, did they? Rick Leon, she noticed, was still sitting alone. All six feet, three inches of him took up two lounge chairs, the second useful for propping the feet and legs. The very *long* feet and legs. Lauren sighed wistfully.

"And he's coming back, right?"

"What? Oh, Neal. Yeah, I guess so. He said he was."

"Then he will. Neal is just about the cutest, nicest boy here. Except maybe for David Hamilton. And he's been out of town all summer."

"Neal *is* cute and he *is* nice," Lauren agreed. "He's also short," she added flatly.

Silly looked shocked. "Lauren! That's so shallow!"

"You wouldn't say that if you were my size," Lauren retorted, annoyed. Were all petite people so judgmental? What did Silly Burke know about never getting to wear high heels? About scrunching your shoulders down inside your sweater or coat in a futile attempt to remove an inch from the top? About feeling like a mutant because you towered over every boy you knew? "If you think Neal is so great, why don't you do something about it?" she suggested.

"I did," Silly said sadly. "He wasn't interested. I have a feeling he thinks my nickname suits me."

Poor Silly. At least no one could do much damage to the name "Lauren." Except use a substitution like "Stilts."

"Here he comes," Silly said breathlessly. "I'd better go. You two have fun!"

Lauren saw Neal approaching and thought again how nice-looking he was. What were the chances that he might grow four inches between that very day and Labor Day weekend? Couldn't all this fresh air and sunshine work some kind of miracle?

Neal was only two tables away when Rick Leon stirred, climbed out of his two lounge chairs, and aimed his long, lanky body straight at Lauren's table.

Chapter 2

Blaine Hamilton shifted impatiently on the bleacher. Why didn't Jeff just finish off this match so they could go to lunch? She was starving. She'd overslept, leaving no time for so much as a doughnut and coffee. Whose idea was it to schedule the match for nine o'clock in the morning, anyway? Probably Jeff's, just to torture her. He knew she was a night person. Not that he cared. All he cared about was tennis! He was perfectly content to *thwoop-thwoop* little yellow-green balls all day long, in spite of a sun that threatened to turn Blaine's skin to shoe leather.

She tossed her head impatiently. Her hair felt like silk. Most of the blondes in Oceanview this late in the summer had hair that looked like old straw hats. Not Blaine's. Anthony had cut her shoulder-length strands, blonde-white from the sun, perfectly this time. And she didn't care how expensive his conditioning treatments were, they were worth it.

Blaine knew she was pretty. Everyone said so,

and her mirror confirmed it. Her features were finely chiseled, her skin flawless, her tan perfect. "An even, glowing bronze" was what the cosmetics salesperson had promised the twenty-dollar tube of lotion would deliver, and an even, glowing bronze was what she had.

It was nice to be pretty. Unlike that girl Jeff was playing this morning, who could certainly do with a makeover. Were all girl athletes so plain? Maybe they didn't care about looks.

"Hi, Blaine," two girls in tank tops and shorts called out, "David back yet?"

If one more girl asked her about her brother, she was going to jump to her feet and scream at the top of her lungs, disrupting the match and causing Jeff, who loved her, to hate her forever. Disrupting his tennis match would be worse than shouting "Fire!" at a rock concert. At least to Jeff it would be.

"David got back last night," she answered curtly, her eyes following the tennis ball, head moving left to right, right to left, like a swinging door caught in a brisk wind.

"Is he coming to the club today?" one of the girls asked eagerly.

She wouldn't scream. She couldn't afford to have Jeff hating her right now, with the Sandcastles Ball coming up. This was no time to lose a boyfriend.

"How should I know?" she said irritably. "Why don't you post a guard at the gate? That way, you'll be alerted the moment my brother arrives."

They giggled uncertainly. But when Blaine refused to look at them or to smile, they shot her a look of disgust and turned away. They were shaking their heads and whispering as they pretended to watch the match. Blaine knew perfectly well what she was being called as they whispered together. She didn't care. Every unattached girl, it seemed to her, had asked about David today. He'd been away, taking some course at a university, something horrid like biology or zoology. Whatever. Now he was back and any girl who wasn't already attached (and some who were, if the truth were known) was on the alert, ready and waiting.

They were wasting their time. David Hamilton had dated every single girl the family knew. Once. Just once. Then he'd dated a group of girls Blaine thought of as "ordinary people," meaning girls the Hamilton family didn't know personally. Also just once. Her brother was obviously looking for someone extraordinary. So far, he hadn't found her.

And those two giggling girls whispering about Blaine had no chance of catching David Hamilton's attention. They were too young, for one thing. And they were too obviously interested in him.

A wild burst of applause from the few scattered spectators startled Blaine. This was a practice, for heaven's sake! Why applaud at practice? Annoyance tugged at her, making her sit up straight and pay attention. Practice or not, Jeff would ask her how he had looked. He always did, even though he knew she cared about this stupid game the way he cared about doing something new and different for a change.

"What's wrong with the way things are now?"

he protested whenever she complained that she was bored. "We don't have to work like a lot of the other kids, we have the whole summer free to spend here at the club, and we've got each other. What's the problem?"

The problem was, this summer would be exactly like last summer. She would buy a dozen or more cute little short-skirted outfits, plant herself in the bleachers while Jeff played tennis until the skin fell off every ball in town, and her head would swing back and forth like the pendulum on the Hamiltons' grandfather clock. On weeknights and weekends, Jeff would really be too pooped from all the tennis to do much dancing. They'd go to the club, anyway, because hope springs eternal, and she'd sit at their table, while Jeff talked tennis with any person he could hold captive, and then they'd go home. Same old thing.

The sound of tires on gravel behind her caught her attention. Blaine's head turned. A large blue van had pulled up at the rear entrance to the club-house. She was about to return her attention to the match when the van's side doors slid open and a young man holding an instrument case jumped down. Guitar case, Blaine decided. A musician.

The van's doors closed and off it went. But the new arrival stayed. Blaine turned her body completely around, away from the match, and boldly stared. He wasn't as good-looking as Jeff or as tall. But he looked . . . interesting. Lean. Lanky. Hair the color of beach sand, worn in a ponytail. Western boots. Jeans. He was standing on the gravel, guitar case in hand, facing the clubhouse entrance. She could see a name on his jeans belt, spelled out in large red stones: DUKE.

If he was looking for a job, she thought, he was wasting his time. The band already had a guitar player.

Had he felt her staring at him? Maybe, because in the next second, his head turned and their eyes met. He grinned and saluted. Blaine, who was never caught off-guard, sent him a sultry smile. But every nerve in her body sprang to attention. This could be interesting. What were her chances of getting the regular guitar player fired? Her parents, Leah and Harper Hamilton, practically ran The Dunes. Shouldn't that count for something? With a guy like this one around, the rest of the long, boring summer could perk up.

With a wave of his hand, he turned and crunched his way across the gravel to the clubhouse door.

Blaine, looking much more alert than she had before the van's arrival, faced the court again. He'd looked older. Eighteen? Nineteen? Twenty, maybe. No problem. She looked a lot older than sixteen. Jeff complained about it all the time. Something about her clothes being "too grown up." Ridiculous. Her clothes were chic and expensive. Could she help it if what was fashionable added a few years to her look?

Musicians were never rich. And this one certainly hadn't looked it. The heels on those cowboy boots weren't what they used to be. And rich was an absolute requirement in anyone Blaine dated. As long as there was ever one rich, single male on the planet, Blaine had no intention of dating a poor one. Those people who said money couldn't buy happiness had never seen her fire-engine red Mercedes-Benz convertible with white sidewalls.

It wasn't as if she was actually thinking about dating the musician. She already had a boyfriend. A rich one. She certainly wasn't crazy enough to dump Jeff Christian for some traveling guitar player with run-down heels.

The plain girl beat Jeff. Hadn't she beat him before? Blaine thought she was some sort of champion. Blaine stood up, fluffed her hair, and smoothed her tiny little yellow skirt, and climbed down the bleachers to go comfort Jeff.

He couldn't possibly know that as she gave him a hug and a kiss, she was thinking of a grin and a salute and a guitar player.

David Hamilton, all six feet, two inches of him, entered the Drifting Dunes dining room and looked around. Sunglasses in hand, he leaned against a thick wooden pillar, waving at the many people calling out greetings to him. He was glad to be home. The course he'd taken had been interesting and worth the time, but he was ready to relax now and gear up for senior year at Woodrow Wilson High School.

The first time he noticed the girl, he almost dropped his sunglasses. Just as he turned away from the pillar, she passed him. He hadn't seen her that clearly, couldn't say, for example, the exact color of her eyes or the length of her eyelashes or whether or not she had a space between her upper front teeth. What he did see was enough to make his breath catch in his throat. Masses of wavy red hair, pulled back and fastened away from a tanned, heart-shaped face. Wide, bright eyes. High cheekbones and a straight, narrow nose. A beautiful girl. The prettiest girl he had ever seen.

But what really caught his attention was the way she moved. Light and fast without seeming to be in a hurry. A white terrycloth robe hung around her shoulders, and as she reached a corner table and put her tray on it, she turned sideways. Under the robe, she was wearing a white one-piece bathing suit, with the word LIFEGUARD superimposed over The Dunes' trademark, two small sand dunes inside an ocean wave.

He had no idea who she was. He had never seen her before.

But he knew one of the waitresses in the dining room. He went over to her. "Jody, who's the red-head?" he asked casually, although to him the question was anything but casual. Maybe the girl was from out of town and, come September, would vanish like a summer tan. Maybe she went steady with a very possessive two hundred and fifty pound gorilla-type.

"That's Shannon Murphy. She lives up the road, in that big yellow house just off the beach." Jody grinned. "Isn't she something? She's nice, too. Everyone likes her." She began ticking off statistics on her fingers: "Not quite sixteen years old. Smart as a whip. Super swimmer. Beach lifeguard. No boyfriend, as far as I know. I haven't seen one."

No boyfriend? *No boyfriend?* He'd had a good summer so far. He was about to have an even better one.

Jody touched his arm. "David, I get the feeling she's not all that comfortable around people like you Hamiltons. So, if what you're looking for is a summer fling, try someone else, okay? I wouldn't want to see this girl get hurt."

Hurt this girl? Never! He shook his head. "Not me," he said emphatically. "I think if all I wanted was a summer fling, as you put it, I could probably come up with something. That's not what I'm looking for." Even as he spoke, three girls in bikinis passed him, smiling an open invitation.

Jody laughed. "Yeah, I guess you're right. It's not as if girls run away when you enter a room. Okay, then, I wish you luck." And she went back to work.

Smiling, David headed for Shannon Murphy's table.

Chapter 3

Shannon Murphy, head bent over her salad, didn't notice the boy approaching her table by the window. If she had, she would have jumped up, grabbed her tray with her barely touched lunch on it, and hurried out of the room before he arrived.

Not because this particular boy was unattractive. This tall, blond, smiling guy in white shorts and a short-sleeved shirt was about as far from unattractive as you could get without reaching unreal. And not because she was already attached to some other guy. She wasn't. Well, not really.

Shannon would have departed hastily because she had sworn off boys for the summer. Maybe forever. And she was sticking to that. She had had enough of boys to last her a long, long time.

First she'd had her hands full with that big-mouth, Charlie Wainwright. It was hard to understand why that boy was so popular. Everyone had approved of them dating, said they made a "cute couple." But dating the life of the party got stale very quickly. Charlie had to have a good time or he went nuts. No quiet sitting on the beach for *this* party animal. That was her favorite thing to do, and Charlie wasn't interested. The word "quiet," he said, made him break out in a cold sweat. He was too loud, too busy, too frantic for her. So she told Charlie she'd see him around.

Then, when Thad Wilcox, a junior at Oceanview High, asked her to dance at one of the spring school dances, she was impressed by his shy, quiet politeness and said yes. And began dating him.

Mistake number two for Shannon Elizabeth Murphy.

Faster than she could say, "Ooops," Thad was calling her on the phone constantly, waiting for her after every class, writing her notes, and arriving unannounced at her house at all hours of the day and night. People began calling him her shadow, and her mother began expressing her annoyance. "Shannon, that boy is driving me nuts!" was what she had said exactly. "*Do* something!"

So Shannon told Thad she wanted to see other people, hoping he would react the same way Charlie had, with a joke and a shrug.

He didn't. No joke. No shrug. He became very upset, asking what he'd done wrong, promising to stop doing whatever it was, and telling her that if he'd made mistakes it was because he loved her so much.

Loved? Now there was a word that people didn't usually toss out into everyday, ordinary conversation. And one she had never used in connection with Thad Wilcox.

It was a horrible scene. Even now, two months later, Shannon shuddered every time she thought about it.

He hadn't given up. He kept sending her things: notes, flowers, drawings of the little "Smiley" with its mouth upside down, tears dripping from little black dot eyes. At first the notes begged her to take him back. But lately, they'd changed. The tone, Shannon thought, had become angrier, almost threatening. The last one said, *"Don't go out with anyone else.* I couldn't stand that."

Well, at least he had stopped begging. She'd hated that. It made her feel guilty, as if she'd slapped an innocent child.

She should have listened to her younger sisters. They hadn't liked Thad. B.J. had said, "He's got pale eyes, Shannon. Like a fish. A dead fish." And Marilyn had said, "He gives me the creeps. He looks at you like he'd chain you to his wrist if he could."

She should have listened to them.

Too late now.

"Hi!" the blond boy said as he arrived at her table. "Okay if I sit?"

"Sure," Shannon said cheerfully. "Help yourself." Then she promptly stood up, reaching down for her tray.

"Hey, wait a minute! You're not leaving, are you?" His eyes, when he looked down at her, were as warm a blue as the water in the pool.

"That's the plan," she answered lightly. She couldn't shake the feeling that Thad was looking over her shoulder. That was just plain silly, as long as she was at The Dunes. Thad never came here. He hated the beach. The ocean terrified him. One of the reasons she'd accepted this job was knowing she'd be free of him at The Dunes.

"You can't leave," the boy said. He was a head taller than Shannon. "We haven't had a chance to talk."

"Sorry. No time." She was not going to bring some poor unsuspecting guy into this awful situation with Thad. Especially not a guy who looked as nice as this one did. That smile could turn solid gold into a puddle of yellow goo. She'd never seen him before. He couldn't be a student at Oceanview High. She'd have noticed him. Maybe he went to Wilson, up on the hill. Probably. That looked like an expensive haircut, and he had a reptile slithering across his shirt pocket.

"Excuse me," she said politely, and turned to walk swiftly toward the door, depositing her tray on the counter as she passed it.

"Wait!" David couldn't believe he was letting her get away. What was wrong with him, anyway? Bad breath? The haircut? He'd had it cut a little shorter this time, thinking it would be cooler that way.

He was being stupid. She couldn't be the kind of girl who would cold-shoulder a guy because of his haircut. That was more his sister Blaine's speed.

He loved the way she moved, so lightly, almost as if she were dancing. There was a kind of natural rhythm to her movements. She was probably a great dancer.

Well, it wasn't as if he didn't know where to find her. She was a beach lifeguard.

Thad Wilcox sat alone at the desk in his room, his sandy, uncombed head bent over a sheet of yellow paper. The orange drapes were pulled shut, the only light in the dim room coming from a small green desk lamp. He muttered to himself as he wrote.

"Thad? Thad!"

His mother. What did she want now? Why couldn't she leave him alone? What he was doing was important. More important than any stupid little errand she might want him to run.

"Thad, you heard your father last night. He wants you to look for a job *today*. He made that very clear." Then, "Thad? Are you listening to me?"

She was calling from downstairs. She wouldn't come up. He knew that. The stairs leading to his attic room were narrow and steep and she hated them. He loved them . . . because she hated them. And that gave him the privacy he wanted.

"Thad, you've already wasted half the summer. You spend too much time up there in that room. You need a job to keep you busy."

He had a job. Why couldn't she understand that? His job was getting Shannon back. That was more important than anything else. That was the *only* thing.

Before answering his mother, he glanced around the room. There were pictures of Shannon Murphy everywhere, pictures she didn't know he had, didn't know he had taken. Expensive camera equipment given him by his parents in the hope that he'd develop an interest in photography had allowed him to photograph Shannon repeatedly without her knowledge. There were pictures of her laughing with friends. He'd cut the friends out after developing the pictures in their basement darkroom. There were pictures of Shannon running; walking with her two younger sisters, whom Thad couldn't stand. Pictures of Shannon coming out of school; going into school; hurrying up the steps to her house. The pictures were the reason he kept his door locked.

His mother wouldn't go away until he answered her. He fixed pale eyes on the door to his room. "Okay, Mom," he called out cheerfully. "This afternoon, I promise."

He had to go out to deliver the letter he was writing, anyway. He'd just tell them at dinner that there weren't any jobs. It didn't matter if they didn't believe him. That wasn't important.

His mother's high heels clicked away from the foot of the stairs and back into the kitchen, the sound fading as she moved.

Satisfied, Thad bent his head over the yellow paper and began to print laboriously. He hated his own penmanship and had begun printing in large black capital letters. It seemed much more impressive to him than sprawled cursive.

YOU HAVE REALLY HURT ME, SHANNON, he wrote.

* * *

Shannon, well-oiled as a protection against the sun's burning rays, was perched atop her high white station, thinking that the only thing she disliked about her job was how little time it allowed her to swim. There were times when she found herself actually hoping someone would begin to flounder in the water, just a little, giving her an excuse to dive into the buoyant, cooling waves. Then she would laugh softly to herself, reprimanding silently, Shannon Murphy, you are a horrible person! Wanting someone to practically drown just so you can get wet. Shame on you!

But the ocean she loved was so tantalizingly close. And it was kind enough to provide a nice, cooling breeze, or she'd have roasted to death. She didn't even mind the occasional dead-fish smell. It was part of the sea, so she accepted it, even as the people lying and sitting on the beach below wrinkled their noses in distaste.

"Shannon Murphy?"

Shannon looked down. The blond boy from the dining room was standing on the sand, looking up.

"Can I come up there?"

He didn't give up easily, did he? He looked like an ad for a California Tourist Bureau campaign. So tan, so blond, so healthy-looking. And so *rich*.

She didn't really have anything against wealthy people. They had a right to live, too. She simply preferred that they do it in their own world. She was only working in theirs.

Then again, Thad Wilcox was from her world,

wasn't he? Ordinary house, ordinary neighborhood, two ordinary parents. Vacation once a year, two cars, both older models, the kids going to college but having to come up with at least part of the tuition. Her family and Thad's were a lot alike.

Except that Thad had never learned how to take "no" for an answer, something she'd learned when she was only four years old and wanted, in the worst way, a pony.

Thad didn't want a pony. He wanted her.

"No, you can't come up," she yelled down to the blond boy. "No one's allowed up here. I'm working."

Shielding his eyes from the sun with his hand, he grinned up at her. "Nice work if you can get it. You don't look very busy."

She wasn't allowed to read or listen to music while on duty. Reading would take her eyes off the water, where they belonged, and music would drown out any cries for help.

"Can I help it if no one is drowning right at the moment?" she said.

She wondered if he knew the fifty-dollar haircut had left a tiny little cowlick pointing straight toward the sky.

He laughed when she said no one was drowning at the moment. "Is that what I have to do to get your attention? Drown?"

When she had started working at The Dunes, more than one boy had faked a drowning as a way of getting her to notice him. That had stopped when they'd all realized how thoroughly disgusted such a stupid stunt made her.

"Drowning isn't funny," she scolded sternly.

"Sorry. You're right. It isn't."

Two young boys were venturing out into the ocean too far. Shannon blew the whistle that hung on a gold chain around her neck, waving the boys back in toward shore. They looked up, straight at her, and continued swimming through the waves, away from the other swimmers.

The whistle shrilled again, more insistently this time. People on the beach looked up with interest. Was something happening?

She would blow the whistle one more time. Then she'd go in after them. They had a major head start on her, but she was so sure of herself in this ocean, she knew she could catch them before they hit serious trouble.

She'd bet anything they were Neal Winthrop's younger brothers. The Titanic Twins — your heart sank every time you saw them. They were mutants, she was sure of it. Poor Neal. The demons had probably been banished from the pool for some major infraction of the rules and had sneaked down to the beach to wreak more havoc. And where was Neal? He'd told her that keeping the "wild animals in check" was his job this summer. It wasn't like him to goof off.

The boys ignored the third and final shrill of her whistle. She was just about to begin the hasty climb downward when the blond boy called, "Sit still! I'll get them!" And before she could stop him, he'd slipped out of his loafers and gone dashing down the beach to fling himself into the waves.

Shannon watched, stunned. And furious. Who did he think he was? This was *her* job! And she wasn't some poor, helpless female who couldn't handle a tricky situation with two small but abominable little boys. She felt incredibly foolish standing on her station, watching, while someone else performed *her* rescue mission. Even if that someone was quite a swimmer.

In minutes, he and the beasts were standing below her, the boys defiant and unabashed, their rescuer beaming with pride.

Livid, Shannon climbed down to face them on the sand.

"You two," she told the boys, "go find your brother. Now! And do not let me see your faces on this beach again while I'm on duty. Understood?"

They nodded, turned, and ran up the beach. She knew they were giggling. And she knew they'd be back. They hadn't taken her seriously. She'd have to talk to Neal about them, and soon!

Then she turned her attention to the sodden but satisfied pseudolifeguard. His white clothes were covered with sand and seaweed. "And you!" she said sharply. "Don't ever do anything like that again! I could be fired for what you just did. *I'm* the lifeguard here and if I need any help, I'll ask for it. Understood?"

He grinned. Extending one wet arm, he said, "Pleased to meet you, Shannon Murphy. My name is David Hamilton. I *am* sorry. I shouldn't have jumped in like that, and if you can forgive me, I'm going to take you to the Sandcastles Ball, Labor Day weekend."

Shannon's mouth dropped open slightly. "I don't even know you."

He began backing away, still smiling. "You will by then," he said, "and that's a promise. See you later. That's a promise, too."

Then he turned and plodded off through the sand, leaving Shannon staring after him.

At 44 Seascape Drive, the large, old yellow house in which Shannon lived with her mother and two younger sisters, a tall, thin boy with stooped shoulders slid a sheet of yellow paper into the black metal mailbox hanging beside the front door. He smiled briefly. It was not a happy smile.

Then he took the wooden steps two at a time, jumped on a waiting bicycle, and pedaled away.

Chapter 4

Ka-thunk! Thwoop! The yellow-green ball collided with Jamie Smith's powerful backhand and went sailing back over the net as if shot from a cannon. She watched it go without satisfaction. Jeff Christian would return it. He was as familiar with her playing style as she was with the ratty old sneakers she was wearing, the ones her father had tried to trash the day before.

"You can't wear those old things forever," he had said when she stubbornly retrieved them from the yellow wastebasket in the kitchen. "They're not good for your feet. Or your game."

"I can't play in new shoes," she'd insisted, knowing it wasn't true. She could play tennis well in fishing boots if she had to. But right then, she needed something warm and known and comfortable on her while she played. The ratty old shoes were all she had. So she clung to them.

" 'Atta girl!" her father shouted now from the sidelines.

But she felt nothing. Jeff would return her shot,

she would return his, he would slam it back to her . . . on and on and on, until finally one of them would break concentration and bobble a return. Probably Jeff. He hadn't beaten her in months.

She had been playing tennis for ten years. Her father had put a tennis racket in her hands on her fifth birthday. It had been there ever since.

"Jamie, wake up!" her father called sharply. The ball had come within a millisecond of passing her by.

Shame on you, she scolded silently, you almost missed a ball! That could mean the end of the world! Whole countries could be wiped out, flood and famine could sweep across the earth, seven deadly plagues might be visited upon us if Jamie Smith actually missed a ball.

"Shape up, Smith!" Jeff called good-naturedly. "Or are you really planning to let me win this one for a change?"

He was so nice. He had reddish-blond curly hair, hazel eyes, and a warm, friendly smile. If she thought losing to Jeff would mean a date with him, she might just let him win.

But he'd never ask her out. She was just a tennis partner to him, nothing more. And besides, he was as much in love with stuck-up Blaine Hamilton as Jamie was with him.

Even if there were no Blaine (and wasn't *that* a lovely thought?), he wouldn't ask her out. Because, she reminded herself, I'm not pretty. I'm healthy, hours in the sun have given me a great tan, and I don't have an ounce of fat on my body. But I'm not pretty. Not even close, and Jeff likes pretty girls . . . girls like Blaine.

Jamie could remember as if it were yesterday overhearing her grandmother talking about her when she was six years old. "It's a good thing you're teaching that child to play tennis," the woman told her son, "because she's going to need *something* to make her feel good about herself. The poor little thing is as plain as a mud fence, and always will be. Anyone can see that."

Jamie could certainly see it. Plain, sharply angled face, cheekbones reddened by sea air and sunshine. Plain brown eyes, with short, straight, pale lashes. Plain, straight brown hair cut shorter than some boys wore theirs. Every time she tried to let it grow out, it flopped across her eyes on the courts and her father barked, "Cut it!" So she did.

Her grandmother was right. She would never be pretty enough for Jeff. Or any other boy.

Well, maybe she wasn't pretty, like Blaine Hamilton, but she was a champion. Dunes Champion. City Champion. County Champion. Champions do not throw matches. If she ever did, all of those trophies sitting in the den at her house would probably disintegrate in disgrace, just disappear into the woodwork as if she'd imagined them into existence in the first place.

Ka-thunk! Thwoop! Back and forth, back and forth . . .

"Good shot!" her father called. Jeff nodded in generous agreement as he raised his arms to slam the ball back to her.

What would they say, Jamie wondered wearily, if I just dropped this racket on the ground and announced that I'm sick to death of playing tennis? Would my father have a stroke? Would Jeff faint?

She was tired of tennis ruling her life. The sun was too hot. The racket, suddenly, had become too heavy. Her elbow ached constantly. The crowds and the noise and the acclaim weren't fun anymore.

She had become a tennis player to please her father. And she had stayed with it because she didn't have anything else in her life that made her feel good. For a long time, her father's praise and approval and the community's pride in her were more than enough.

But not now. Now, she wanted something more in her life. She wanted some of the things other girls had, like dates and parties and someone special telling her there was more to her than just a super backhand. She had begun to hear *ka-thunk* in her dreams. Her sweet, romantic dreams of Jeff turned into nightmares in which she was standing knee-deep in quicksand, reaching out to a distant Jeff with arms that had tennis rackets growing out of her wrists where her hands should have been.

Most of all, after years of hard work, and so many championships won, and so many trophies in the den of her house, she was tired of always, *always* being expected to win.

"Jamie, wake up!" her father shouted. "You're losing control of the ball!"

Wasn't it just terribly convenient that her father was the tennis pro at Drifting Dunes Beach and

Tennis Club? That way, she didn't even have to take a bus to the club every day; she just rode along with him. Lucky her. Of course, if her father wasn't a tennis pro in the first place, she wouldn't even be playing tennis.

"Jamie! Put some power behind that backhand! What's with you today?"

Jamie do this, Jamie do that. Tote that barge, hit that ball! What will happen to me, she wondered as she raced to the net, if I give up tennis? Will I just disappear from the face of the earth? If there is no Tennis Champion Jamie Smith, will Jamie Smith cease to exist?

Poor Daddy, she thought as she slammed a mean one back to Jeff. He wanted a boy. Well, she had tried hard to give him what he wanted. What scared her now was the possibility that she had succeeded too well. Because she certainly didn't feel much like a girl. Not much like a girl at all.

Ka-thunk! Might as well get this stupid practice match over with. *Thwoop!* She gave it all she had.

"That's it!" her father cried triumphantly, running to her side, towel in hand. "The Champeen wins again."

Jamie wiped her sweat-streaked face. "It was just practice, Dad."

He threw an arm around her shoulders as they left the court. Jeff walked beside them, racket over his shoulder. "There's no such thing as just practice, baby," her father reminded her. "You looked a little weak out there in the backhand department. I think maybe we should do this again this afternoon. I have a couple of hours free. Jeff? That suit your schedule?"

Jeff glanced up at the bleachers. Blaine was there, about to come down and meet him. He'd promised her if she came to watch this morning, he'd do something fun with her after lunch. But he and Jamie had that doubles tournament coming up soon. How could he pass up the chance for a little extra practice just to lounge around the pool or play cards or Ping-Pong in the clubhouse? Blaine would just have to understand.

He knew she wouldn't. She'd get that pouty look on her face, the one in which her beautiful blue eyes turned cold as ice and her mouth slid down at the corners. He hated it when she got like that. And sometimes it took days before she was friendly again.

He loved Blaine. They'd known each other forever. She was the prettiest, sexiest girl he knew and he felt lucky to have her. And when she was in a good mood, she was a lot of fun. But when she didn't get her own way, she had tantrums just like a little kid. He was in no mood for one of those tantrums now, but practicing was important.

Just as he was about to announce his agreement to the afternoon session, Jamie said calmly but clearly, "No."

"No?" her father said. "No, what?"

"No, I'm not practicing this afternoon." She couldn't believe she had actually said it. She hadn't intended to. It had just slipped out, as if it could no longer tolerate being kept prisoner inside her head.

Their little group of three had stopped in front of the bleachers. Jamie noticed Blaine making her way down toward them. Oh, terrific! If she argued with her dad in front of Blaine Hamilton, every word would circulate throughout the club faster than the salty ocean breeze. Gossip was to Blaine what tennis was to Jeff. Only Blaine's little yellow-green balls were rumors, served with a power any athlete would envy.

But Jamie wasn't willing to back down. She was asking for so little . . . just an afternoon, that was all. One tiny little afternoon. She deserved to have that for herself.

"Why not?" her father wanted to know as Blaine joined them. Her hair, face, and figure struck Jamie as being absolutely perfect.

Reminding herself that Blaine was only perfect on the outside, Jamie told her father, "I . . . I have plans." She felt a painful flush stealing up from inside the collar of her white one-piece tennis dress. Her palms were sweaty, her stomach churning. But this was important.

"Plans? What kind of plans?" Her father looked honestly puzzled.

Well, he probably *was* confused. Because she had never *had* plans before. Thinking quickly, she said, "I have to go shopping. For shoes."

Her father laughed. "Don't tell me you're finally going to ditch those wrecks you're wearing. I told you you couldn't play in them."

Everyone's eyes went straight to Jamie's feet. Blaine laughed.

"No," Jamie said. "I'm not going shopping for tennis shoes. I'm going shopping for a pair of pumps." She smiled at her father. "White ones, I think."

"Pumps? You're missing practice for a pair of shoes you'll probably never wear? You can't be serious."

A giddy laugh nearly escaped Jamie's lips. Did he mean she wasn't allowed to be serious about a pair of white pumps, as in, "You can't play in the street"? Was there a law on the books somewhere in this state forbidding a fifteen-year-old tennis champion to be serious about anything except her sport? Anything as frivolous, say, as a pair of white pumps? And what did he mean, she would never wear them? Was he pointing out that she had never had a date and wasn't likely to?

No. Her father wasn't cruel. He must have meant she wouldn't have time to wear them. Sure. That was almost certainly what he'd meant.

"Daddy," she said quietly. "I'm not practicing this afternoon. Maybe tonight, when it cools off a little. But this afternoon, I am going shopping." She hesitated and then added, just as quietly, "And you might have asked me if I had time to practice. You asked Jeff."

Then she told Jeff she'd see him later and hurried off to the showers.

Chapter 5

Lauren Tolliver had had more than one daydream about boys. Not one of them had included two cute boys approaching her at exactly the same moment.

Because Neal stopped to answer a question from one of the groups seated at a table, Rick was the first to arrive. He leaned over the table, placing his hands on the blue-checked cloth, and grinned down at her. His eyebrows were as dark as his hair, his eyes hazel. His lower teeth, she noticed, were a little crooked in front, giving him a slightly rakish look.

He wasted no time. "How about a movie tonight?" he asked her.

"A movie?" She could walk into the theater with this boy without scrunching her shoulders down or bending her knees. "I'd love it!"

"Great! Pick you up at seven." He stood up straight. Six feet three if he was an inch!

Wasn't The Dunes the greatest place in the world? "See you then," she said. But he didn't leave.

What was he waiting for? Had she forgotten something?

"It would help," he said lazily, "if I had your address."

Lauren felt her cheeks blazing with embarrassment. What a ninny! "Oh. Sorry. Forty-four North Prospect Street," she said hastily.

"Right. Be ready, okay?" He turned and ambled off, his hands in the pockets of his denim cut-offs.

Neal, tray in hand, arrived just as Rick rounded a corner up ahead. "You know Rick?" he asked, handing her a cup.

"Not really." But I *will*, she thought happily. Then, telling herself that it wasn't polite to think about one boy while you were with another, she said sincerely, "Thanks for the cool wet stuff."

"No problem." He sat down beside her. She decided it wasn't too bad as long as they were seated, especially when she slid down slightly in her chair, resting her head against its back. No one passing by could tell that her growth hormones outraced his.

Maybe they could make a pact, promising never to stand up while they were together. Lauren almost laughed aloud, thinking of the strain *that* would put on a relationship.

They began discussing the band hired by The Dunes (both liked it). And then they moved on to music in general (he liked classical, she preferred rock). They were deep in conversation when two small but sturdy tornadoes came hurtling toward them and threw themselves into the two empty white chairs. The twins had returned.

"Oh, great!" Neal cried, "the missing links! Perfect timing, as usual. Where have you two been? Teasing small animals and babies?" To Lauren, he said, "Meet my brothers, Matt and Mart. The perpetrators of your downfall earlier today. The famous _diving board incident?"

Lauren nodded without smiling. Two blond, bronzed, small people sat opposite her, angelic grins on their little round faces.

"I think you owe this nice lady an apology," Neal told the twins sternly. "She's the one you sent sailing off the high board today."

"We're sorry," they said in one matter-of-fact voice. "We didn't see you."

"Probably because I'm so tiny," Lauren said drily, sitting up very straight.

"Wow!" Mart said, brown eyes like Neal's opened very wide, "you're *enorm*ous! How come you like my brother? He's a lot shorter than you."

Someday, Lauren thought, they might very well be nice and smart and kind, like Neal. But not now. Maybe someone could just lock them in their room until they were civilized. Wasn't the law supposed to protect the populace from public nuisances? Didn't these two give new meaning to the word "nuisance"?

"You've been down on the beach!" Neal accused, picking at bits of seaweed clinging to one boy's trunks. "I told you, no more swimming!"

"You said we had to stay away from the pool," Matt protested. "And we did!"

"Yeah," Neal grumbled as he stood up, "and I'll bet anything you went out too far in the ocean."

The twins traded guilty glances.

"Right," Neal said wearily, "and I'll bet Shannon had to go out after you. I'll hear about *that*. I promised her — "

"No," Matt interrupted truthfully, "Shannon got to stay in her chair the whole time. Honest, Neal!" Being intelligent little boys, they left out the part about David Hamilton diving in after them.

"Look," Neal told Lauren, "I've got to make The Dunes safe for all humankind by removing these two from the premises. Would you consider taking in a movie with me later?"

"Tonight?" Maybe he meant tomorrow night. Or next week. Or next year, when he'd grown four more inches.

"Yeah, if you're free."

Mart tugged on Neal's arm. "Gosh, Neal," he said with disgust, "don't ask *her* out. She's too tall! You'll look really gross walking around with her. And everybody knows you're my brother."

Neal laughed. "You're worried about *me* embarrassing *you*? That's a switch!" To Lauren, he said, "So, how about it? You willing to take a chance on looking really gross?"

It was hard to believe that she actually agreed with the menacing little monster attached to Neal's arm, but she did. Neal was very nice. But she wasn't about to pass up the chance to look *up* on a date, for a movie with someone who, as Mart had pointed out, was too short for her.

"I'm sorry, Neal," she said, meaning it more than she'd thought she would. "I'm busy tonight."

"See?" Mart proclaimed triumphantly, "*she* thinks you're too short, too."

"I'm telling the truth," Lauren said quietly. "I *am* sorry, and I *am* busy tonight."

"Yeah, sure!" Matt said snidely.

Neal ignored him. "Look, we'll get together another night, okay?" he said to Lauren. "Now, I'm going to do the human race a favor and take these two home. Thanks for the great company. See you!"

Lauren smiled as he left, one twin attached to each hand. No one had ever called her "great company." It sounded nice.

Lauren was thinking as she walked toward the bus stop, I could have suggested to Neal that we take in a movie tomorrow night. Then he would have known for sure that I wasn't turning him down because of how tall he isn't.

So why hadn't she suggested another night? Lauren kicked her bare foot at the sand along the path. Was Silly right? Was she shallow? Was she mean and unfeeling?

She didn't want to be. But maybe when you let things like height or weight or color of hair or eyes get in the way of how you felt about someone, you became shallow and unfeeling. She would have to think about that.

But in the meantime, she had a date that night with a tall person.

So she was smiling as she slid into her sandals and climbed aboard the bus.

Jamie Smith, in cut-offs and a yellow T-shirt and sandals, wandered through the Oceanview Mall fighting with herself about what kind of shoes to buy. Her father was right: where would she ever wear white pumps? It wasn't as if she went dancing. She'd made him mad at her for nothing. Buying a new pair of tennis shoes would cancel out his annoyance with her. And everything would be okay again.

Except that there wouldn't be any nice, shiny, white pumps sitting on the floor of her closet, where she could pick them up and hold them every once in a while and wonder what it was like to be a girl who wore shoes like that.

Tired of arguing with herself, Jamie decided to table the discussion long enough to enjoy an ice-cream cone. She never worried about gaining weight. Impossible, when she spent ninety percent of her life racing back and forth under a hot sun. What the exercise left on, the heat melted off.

The boy behind the ice-cream counter was only a few inches taller than she, and his dark eyes behind wire-rimmed glasses were friendly. He was as lean as she was. Did that mean he played, too? She had to bite her tongue to keep from blurting out, "Tennis, anyone?"

"You're Jamie Smith, aren't you?" he asked as she surveyed her thirty-one flavor choices. "The tennis player."

No, she wanted to reply, I'm Jamie Smith, the *girl*. "I play tennis," she said coolly. "And my name is Jamie Smith. But I'm not *the* tennis player. Lots of people play tennis. I'm just one of them. I'd like Double-Fudge Chocolate, please. In a sugar cone. Two scoops." Why not live it up? This was her day off.

"Oh, you're *not* just one of them," the boy said. "You're the best. Everyone in town knows that."

His dark hair was cut very short. A restaurant rule, probably, Jamie decided. Something to do with sanitary conditions. Some boys would look goofy with short hair. But not this one. It looked good on him.

Looking good or not, she was beginning to get annoyed with him. She was here for ice cream, not tennis talk. She could get that any time, any place. It was ice cream and ordinary conversation that she had to hunt for.

And then he said as he handed her the cone, "Me, I don't know zilch about tennis. It looks hot and boring to me, and very tiring."

Jamie smiled. Her narrow, tanned face lit up. Her brown eyes began to sparkle. Deep pink color appeared high on her cheekbones, a color that came from a feeling of pleasure. He knew nothing about tennis? How wonderful!

"Wow!" the boy said, "that's some smile! You should do that more often."

"If you tell me your name," she said happily, "I'll do it again." She thought with astonishment, I'm flirting! I am actually flirting with this boy.

He laughed. "Alex Krueger. I'm a senior at Oceanview High, and I've never been to a tennis match in my life." He frowned. "That wouldn't be a problem for you, would it?" He looked away shyly and then looked back at her. "I mean, maybe you prefer to be with people who talk tennis all the time."

Jamie thought for a minute. It certainly sounded like this boy was interested in getting to know her better. My goodness, hadn't *that* happened quickly? She'd only come in for an ice-cream cone!

"No," she said firmly, "that would *not* be a problem." She had a strong feeling that none of this was real, that she was actually asleep at home, lost deep inside a dream. Well, it would be very disappointing when she awoke in her room. But for now, she was going to enjoy every minute of what seemed to be happening to her. Not only was she laughing and talking and flirting with this nice male person, but he had just implied that he was interested in dating her. If it was a dream, it was almost the best one she'd ever had.

"So," he said, "if I asked you to the band concert in the park tomorrow night, you wouldn't shoot me down?"

Not unless the hot sun has turned my brain to toast, she answered silently. Aloud, she said, "I'd love to go to the band concert with you. I could meet you at the band shell. Eight o'clock?"

Another frown. "Shouldn't I pick you up?"

No! Her father would begin quizzing him about tennis, and the minute he found out how little Alex knew about the game he'd decide Jamie shouldn't date him.

"That's okay," she assured him, pulling a paper napkin from the metal holder on the counter. "I have a match there in the afternoon, so I'll already be close by." No point in adding that the minute the match ended, she'd be racing home to shower and try to do something with her miserable hair. "See you then. 'Bye!"

Cone in hand, she walked out of the store as if she were walking on soft, fluffy clouds. So *that* was how it happened! When you least expected it, and you weren't even looking for it, someone came along and asked you for a date. Just like that. How weird!

Maybe he had just asked her out because he thought she was famous, at least in Oceanview. Forget the bad thoughts, she scolded. He seemed nice and he was cute, even if he wasn't Jeff Christian. She was going to that band concert with Alex Krueger, and she was going to have a wonderful time.

And for a summer band concert, she decided, she could certainly use a pair of white pumps. Maybe a new sundress, too, something in pale yellow or powder blue to set off her tan.

Quickly munching through her cone, she wiped her mouth with the napkin, tossed it in the trash receptacle and, head high, walked briskly to the nearest department store.

After Shannon Murphy had showered, hung her whistle on a hook inside her locker, and changed into white jeans and a pink crop-top, she left The Dunes employee locker room. She found David Hamilton waiting outside for her.

"Hi!" he said cheerfully. "Need a lift home?"

She was tempted. It had seemed like an awfully long day. She was tired.

But Thad might be waiting for her, probably hiding behind a bush or a parked car. He'd surprised her more than once when she was returning home from work. She had no idea what he'd do if he saw her with another boy.

"No, thanks!" she said lightly. "I've got my bike. And I need the exercise after sitting most of the day."

The salty air was cool, the moon hidden behind a few frothy clouds, as Shannon and David walked to the bicycle rack.

"I could follow along in my car," he offered. "Make sure you get home safely." He grinned. "Who knows what evil lurks out there in the dark?" he said, gesturing with one hand toward the road.

If you only knew, she thought. "I'm used to riding home alone. And I have lights on my bike." She unfastened the lock and jumped on the red-and-silver bicycle. "Thanks anyway. 'Bye." And she pedaled away.

He called after her, "Will you be here tomorrow?"

She didn't answer.

There was no sign of Thad when she got home. But her heart sank as she pulled her bicycle up the steps to park it on the porch, because the corner of a piece of yellow paper hung over the edge of the mailbox. Another one! When would Thad stop writing these pathetic letters?

She wouldn't read it. She'd just tear it into tiny

little pieces and toss it into the wastebasket.

No. That might be foolish. She needed to read it because she needed to know what was going on in his head. It was the only way she had of protecting herself right now.

Sure that Thad was watching her, Shannon removed the letter and took it into the house, locking the front door securely behind her.

Inside, she said hello to her mother and B. J. and Marilyn, who were watching television in the living room, and then continued on down the narrow hallway to the kitchen. Flipping on the overhead fluorescent light, she sank into a wooden straight-backed chair and began to read the heavy black printing on the yellow paper.

> YOU HAVE REALLY HURT ME, SHANNON. YOU HAVE TO COME BACK TO ME. WE BELONG TOGETHER. I CAN'T WAIT FOREVER. IF I HAVE TO MAKE YOU COME BACK TO ME I WILL BECAUSE THAT'S THE RIGHT THING. AND I CAN DO IT BECAUSE I'M STRONG.
>
> I LOVE YOU.
> THAD.

Love? He didn't know the first thing about love. She had to do something about him. But what?

Chapter 6

Blaine Hamilton nearly choked on her asparagus at dinner that night when her father turned to his wife, Leah, and said, "By the way, dear, John had to hire a new guitar player for the club band."

Quickly gulping a drink of water, Blaine devoted all of her attention to her parents' conversation. Visions of cowboy boots and sandy hair danced in her head.

"George Humphrey is ill," her father continued. "Don't know what it is exactly, but his wife tells me he won't be able to join us at the club for the remainder of the summer."

George Humphrey had played guitar at The Dunes since Blaine was seven years old. Her heart did double-time. Ask Father who he hired, she telegraphed mentally to her mother.

"Who is taking his place?" Leah Hamilton asked.

Thank you, Mother. Blaine knew if *she* had expressed curiosity, David would have given her an across-the-table look that said, What are you up to now, sister dear? Who needed that?

"A distant cousin of John's." John was The Dunes' manager. "Travels around a lot. Young man. Haven't met him yet, but John assures me he's quite good. Name is King or Duke, something like that."

A faint grin played on Blaine's lips. DUKE — the red fake-stone letters on the belt. The guy she had assumed was long gone from Oceanview was going to be spending the rest of the summer there. Things were looking up.

"What are *you* grinning about?" David asked suspiciously. "You're not in the market for a traveling musician, are you?"

David liked Jeff. But then, Blaine thought, who didn't? Her parents thought he was perfect for her. Which he would be — if she were yellow-green or white and bounced. Then he'd never leave her side.

"Maybe I just like the idea of new blood in the band," she said lightly. "Especially young blood. Maybe this Duke or King or whatever can get them to stop playing that old 'Good Night, Ladies' at the end of every dance."

Leah Hamilton's lovely face registered shock. "Blaine, darling, that song is traditional."

"Sometimes," Blaine said deliberately, "traditional just means old. Old-fashioned. Outdated. Passé."

"I like it," David said mildly. "It means we can always count on the last dance being a slow one. That's the only way to end a dance."

Blaine shot him an annoyed look. "Why should you care? You don't even have a girlfriend."

He grinned. "That could change any moment

51

now. You never really know what's going to happen from one minute to the next, do you?"

"I don't have time for riddles," Blaine said. "Jeff will be here any minute." She excused herself and ran upstairs to change into a blue silk blouse and matching slacks. Not the sort of thing she usually wore to the club, but then, tonight wasn't a usual sort of night, was it?

So David had found someone, had he? That made her nervous. If it was someone from their crowd, she would have received a phone call from the girl by now. And if it wasn't . . . well, if it wasn't someone she knew, she wasn't interested. And David shouldn't be, either. She'd have to keep an eye on him. He'd been weird ever since he'd talked their parents into letting him attend public high school.

Putting her brother on a mental back burner, she swept her hair high on top of her head, fastening the thick mass with several gold combs. Jeff didn't like her hair this way. But then, it wasn't Jeff she wanted to impress that night.

Her spirits remained high in spite of the fact that Jeff, when he picked her up, complained about being tired.

"So what else is new?" Blaine asked nonchalantly. She didn't care if he fell asleep in the middle of the dance floor tonight. There was new blood at The Dunes and she was interested in it. "You played tennis today, right?"

"Sure."

"Well, you're always beat when you play tennis. And you always play tennis. So you're always beat."

Jeff looked hurt, his lower lip thrusting forth like an unhappy child's. "You aren't the most sympathetic person in the world, Blaine. And I don't see why we have to go to the club every single night."

"Because you ignore me all day," she snapped. "What's fair is fair. You love tennis, so you play all day. I love dancing, so we dance all night. Sounds fair to me."

"But you don't have to play tennis tomorrow. You can sleep all day if you want to. My game is off from so much nightlife."

"Look, Jeff," Blaine said coldly, "why don't you just turn this car around and take me home? I'll drive myself to the club. And you can go home and sleep or practice or whatever it is you need to do to strike terror into the hearts of tennis players everywhere."

Jeff was tempted. His body felt as if it had just gone twelve rounds against a heavyweight boxing champion. All he wanted to do was lie down, but Blaine looked so beautiful. Letting her go to The Dunes alone would be asking for trouble. Sometimes even when she was with him, she sent out signals to other guys. He ignored that because *he* was the one with her.

"I'm fine," he said staunchly. "A few dances and I'll be good as new."

Blaine knew better. But since her thoughts were already centered on someone else, she let it drop.

The Surf Room at The Dunes, smaller and cozier than the ballroom, had been freshly painted in the spring, in sealike shades of turquoise. Its wooden pillars and window trim boasted a warm cream color. Round tables situated along the walls were covered with floor-length turquoise or cream cloths, and the room was lighted by one fat crystal hurricane lamp in the center of each table. Each lamp was encircled with a wreath of fresh miniature roses the color of salmon. The tall, narrow windows were uncovered, providing views of the sea and sky until dark, when outside lights shone out across the water. Two sets of cream-colored French doors led to wide wooden decks overlooking the beach.

Blaine's eyes zeroed in on the guitar player seconds after she stepped into the Surf Room. He was impossible to miss. The denim jacket had been replaced by a tweed sportcoat, and although he was wearing a white shirt and tie, every other member of the band was wearing a conservative dark suit, while Duke was in jeans.

Blaine decided that was fine with her. She wanted someone different, and he was definitely different.

"Let's dance," she said, tugging on Jeff's hand. It seemed like the easiest way to get close to the bandstand. Would Duke remember her?

"The dance floor's too crowded," Jeff complained, his eyes searching the crowd for Jamie. He wanted to ask her about his backhand. She sometimes came to these Saturday night things with her parents. But he didn't see her. "Anyway, I need to sit for a few minutes, to get my energy level up."

"It's a *slow* dance, Jeff," Blaine said sarcastically. "How much energy can it take?" She yanked him forward. "We'll dance around the edges of the crowd." They would reach the bandstand faster that way. "C'mon, quit being such a slug!"

Moving as if his feet were coated with molasses, Jeff obeyed.

Lauren Tolliver had tried on every outfit in her closet. Nothing worked. Nothing she owned seemed to go with anything else she owned. Her favorite blue sweater had a snag in the left elbow (probably, she thought guiltily, from draping it over the floor lamp beside her desk). Lauren had many fine qualities. Everyone said so. Neatness wasn't one of them. Her pink silk shirt was one giant wrinkle with sleeves. Her best designer jeans, sloppily hanging out of an overstuffed dresser drawer, looked as if they'd taken a trip through a food processor. A full khaki skirt with huge pockets boasted one big, fat pizza stain on a pocket, and her tan pleated trousers were worn in one knee.

She was getting desperate. It was late. Any second now, tall, dark, handsome (and impatient?) Rick Leon would be ringing the doorbell. She couldn't very well go in her bathrobe. It had coffee stains on both sleeves.

She settled on white slacks miraculously free of stains and wrinkles, and a red sheer short-sleeved blouse over a white-turtleneck T-shirt. She looked okay. No, she looked *good*. She looked better in blue, but . . . red was more exciting than blue, wasn't it?

Lauren hated the first few minutes of a date with

a new person. She always felt as if she was taking an exam. If she said the right things, she'd get an A and the boy would ask her out again. But if she messed up and got an F, it was bye-bye boy. Sometimes she didn't care. But tonight she did. Because unless Rick turned out to be a total jerk, she wanted to see him again, as in Labor Day weekend, as in the Sandcastles Ball, as in dancing a slow dance with a tall person.

"Heard any good tall jokes lately?" she asked him with a grin as they left her house for the movie theater. It seemed a good idea to point out right away what they had in common. "Establishing a common bond" was the way an article in a popular magazine had put it. It was certainly worth a try.

When she glanced over at him in the front seat of his car, she had to raise her glance to meet his. It felt wonderful.

He returned her grin. "Well, let's see. Heard the one about the guy who was so tall, people in hiking boots climbed him just because he was there?"

Lauren laughed. "No, but I heard the one about the girl who was so tall, air traffic controllers had to reroute the planes in her path."

"Ever get tired of people asking you how the weather is up there?"

Lauren nodded. "And what planet I'm from, and if I've thought about becoming a fireman because I'd never need a ladder, and do birds nest in my hair . . . you name it, I've heard it."

Rick shrugged as they pulled up in front of the

theater. "Nobody bothers me about it much since I started playing basketball."

"I play basketball, too," Lauren said, climbing out of the sedan. "But it doesn't help." Probably, she thought, because the girls' games had very few spectators. Hardly anyone knew she'd been high scorer the season before.

But none of that mattered tonight. Because tonight she was just one of a *pair* of tall people. No one would tease her with Rick at her side. She had never walked so tall and straight as she did as they went into the theater.

Lauren was disappointed in the movie, a cloak-and-dagger thriller with an abundance of violence. Rick seemed to like it. He said it gave him an appetite, and led her to a restaurant a short distance from the theater.

They ran out of conversation halfway through their hamburgers. They had analyzed, dissected, and discussed basketball, and shared every joke they knew. Lauren frantically searched for topics of conversation.

Books?

"Who has time to read?" Rick asked. "That's for couch potatoes."

Music?

"I like the 'rap' stuff," he said, and proceeded to mark time on the tabletop with his fork as he recited one of his favorites. She decided Rick could use a little help with his timing.

So much for music. Maybe they could talk about

The Dunes. After all, that was where they had met.

"I love the colors they painted the Surf Room," she said.

He didn't even look up from his French fries. "They painted the Surf Room?"

She gave up. She had wanted a tall date. She *had* a tall date. Wanting brilliant conversation was probably asking too much. Greed was not nice.

When he took her home, he said, "So. You'll be at the club tomorrow? How about we shoot some hoops?"

Not the most thrilling invitation she'd ever had. But it wouldn't hurt her to practice a little. Summer was almost over and she'd spent a lot more hours in the pool than she had on the basketball court. Coach wouldn't be pleased.

"Sure," she agreed, "why not?"

But she couldn't help wondering, as she went into the house without a good-night kiss, if Rick Leon had approached her table that morning because he was looking for a basketball buddy. Maybe when he'd spotted her he hadn't seen "pretty" or "interesting" or "sexy." Maybe, like so many other boys, he'd only seen "tall."

No, that was silly. Rick had tons of basketball buddies. She had seen him with them, on the court behind the clubhouse.

Teasing herself with the thought that Rick had maybe read the same article she had on "forging relationships with a common bond," in this case an interest in basketball, Lauren went to bed.

Chapter 7

Blaine had no trouble maneuvering an unenthusiastic Jeff toward the bandstand. And no trouble catching Duke's eye. The other girls her age were dressed in white or pastel-colored slacks with casual tops. Blaine was the only one in blue silk and high-heeled sandals. It was a guaranteed way of getting attention.

She smiled at Duke over Jeff's shoulder. He smiled back. Content, Blaine let Jeff dance her away from the bandstand.

Escaping Jeff later was easy. When he started talking tennis with a friend of his, she knew she wouldn't be missed. She walked straight to the bandstand. When she got there, she leaned against the wall, arms folded against her chest, eyes on Duke as he strummed vigorously, his eyes closed.

She didn't have long to wait. The orchestra leader called a break shortly after she arrived. Duke stepped down from the bandstand, guitar in hand, and joined her.

"I'm Blaine Hamilton," she said brightly, hand

extended. "My parents sort of run this place." Deciding that that sounded as if they *worked* there, she amended that impression by adding, "I mean, they're on the Board of Trustees."

He looked unimpressed. But he took her hand. "Duke," he said lazily.

Electricity seemed to zap through Blaine's hand. Her fingertips tingled. And his eyes wouldn't let go of hers. "Meet me after," he commanded softly. It wasn't a question.

She nodded. He turned and moved away.

For a moment, she wondered if she'd imagined the encounter. Deciding she hadn't, she returned to Jeff, her step noticeably lighter than it had been during the previous weeks of summer.

Noticeable to all but Jeff Christian, lost in a discussion about athletes and Vitamin C.

Blaine was patient for a record-breaking six minutes. Then she grabbed Jeff's hand, stopping him in mid-sentence, and said, "If you don't dance with me right this very second, I'm going to make my father cancel your membership here." She wanted the evening to end swiftly, so that she could meet Duke. The fastest way she knew to speed things up was to keep busy, and that did *not* include sitting quietly and talking.

Jeff grumbled, but he knew better than to argue with Blaine.

Every time they danced past the bandstand, which Blaine engineered as often as possible, she smiled at Duke. He seemed to be as lost in his music as Jeff was in tennis. Blaine sighed petulantly.

Wasn't there a boy anywhere who would be interested only in *her?*

Oh, well. At least she had two who were partly interested in her. That was more than many girls had.

She danced the night away with Jeff, counting the minutes until she could meet Duke.

The wall telephone behind Shannon rang. Up to her elbows in dishwashing detergent, she waited for B.J. or Marilyn to answer the ring. Then she remembered: her mother had taken her sisters out for ice cream.

Wiping her hands on a red-striped towel, Shannon picked up the receiver and said impatiently, "Hello?"

"Did you get my letter?"

Thad! She had given strict orders to her mother and sisters to tell him she wasn't home when he called. Honesty might be the best policy with normal people, but not with someone like Thad.

But her family wasn't home to answer the phone now.

"Yes, I got it," she said curtly. She had read somewhere that the best way to get rid of a persistent salesman was out-and-out rudeness. Wasn't Thad a persistent salesman? He was trying to sell himself.

Well, she wasn't buying. "Leave me alone, Thad. I mean it!"

"No, you don't. You couldn't." Pause. Then, "You're not going out with someone else, are you?"

An image of a tall, blond boy in white shorts, a boy with a dynamite smile, appeared briefly on the wall opposite Shannon. She shooed it away. "That's none of your business," she said crisply. But a tiny voice inside her head warned her to be careful. No point in upsetting him. "No, I'm not going out with someone else. I'm too busy."

Silence. She should hang up. Every minute on the phone with him was another minute of his hold on her. Why couldn't he just let go, the way other people did? Normal people, like good old life-of-the-party Charlie.

"I've got to go," she said after moments of tense silence. "Please don't call here again, Thad. Go find some other girl. There are lots of them in Oceanview."

"Not for me, there aren't," he said fiercely. "And I *will* call again. You'll change your mind, Shannon. I'll make you change your mind!"

The click as he replaced the receiver did not seem final to Shannon. Not final at all.

She returned to her dishwater, cold now. She was adding fresh hot water when the phone shrilled again.

I won't answer it, she thought. But there was another ring. In the beginning, Thad's persistence had simply annoyed her, like a pesky mosquito darting in and out of her daily life. But persistence was one thing, while threats were something else again. She should tell someone. But who? Her mother would think she was imagining things. Thad had always been so polite and nice around Mrs. Murphy. She would never believe he had actually threatened her daughter.

The ringing stopped.

Shannon finished the dishes, thinking as she scrubbed and rinsed. Had Thad actually threatened her? It was probably just talk. Whatever it was, he had no business asking her about other boys.

When the phone rang again, her anger, simmering steadily, erupted. Yanking the receiver from its resting-place on the wall, she barked, "Leave me *alone!* I mean it!"

And a voice totally unlike Thad's said, "Guess I caught you at a bad time. Want me to call back later?"

Shannon smiled. The boy in the white shorts. Hamilton. David Hamilton. The one who had fished the Titanic Twins out of the ocean.

Weak with relief and feeling very foolish, Shannon laughed shakily. "Oh, it's you. Sorry. I didn't mean to bite off your head. I've . . . we've been getting crank calls lately. I thought you were one."

"You should file a complaint," David said seriously. "With the telephone company. They might be able to trace one of the calls and find out who the weirdo is."

She wasn't about to tell him the "weirdo" was someone she'd dated. "I'll talk to my mother about it." But she knew she wouldn't.

"Feel like talking, now that you know it's just normal old me?"

Talking to a normal person might take away the memory of Thad's unpleasant phone call. "What about?" she asked.

They were still talking when B.J. and Marilyn, arguing the merits of Mint Chocolate Chip ice cream versus Raspberry Cream Ripple, burst in through the back door. B.J., noticing Shannon on the phone, shushed her sister.

Shannon and David had talked about school, hers in town, his up on the hill. They'd talked about the club and the beach and about a movie newly arrived at Cinema Four in the mall. And they'd laughed a lot, erasing the last of Shannon's tension.

But when David offered to take Shannon to the new movie, the memory of Thad's phone call slammed a barrier down in front of "Yes, I'd love to." Thad had asked if she was seeing someone else. She had truthfully said no. What would he have done if she'd said, "Yes, I am?"

"I'm sorry," she said, "but I can't."

He waited. When she added nothing more, he said lightly, "That's it? You can't go? Nothing about shampooing your hair or doing your nails or an out-of-town cousin coming for a visit?"

Shannon laughed. B.J., standing at the sink, shot her a curious glance.

"You just find me repulsive, is that it?" he said. "Go ahead, tell me the truth. I can take it."

Snakes were repulsive. Lima beans were repulsive. Ditto mint-gel toothpaste. But David Hamilton was *not* repulsive. Not even close.

"No, that's *not* it," she said earnestly. "This is really just a bad time for me, that's all. My mother has been tutoring people who can't read, and when she's not home evenings I stay with my younger sisters."

B.J. glared at her. She and Marilyn had stayed by themselves many evenings since B.J. turned twelve and Marilyn ten. They preferred it that way, probably convinced that having an older sister around would spoil their mischief. They were never afraid of being alone at night. But it was the only excuse that came to Shannon's mind.

"Oh," David said. "Well, I hate to brag, but I'm pretty good with little kids, if you need some help."

Shannon grinned at B.J., standing five feet, six inches tall in her flat-heeled sandles. Marilyn wasn't more than an inch shorter. These "little kids" would be livid if they'd overheard David's description of them.

"Thanks," she said. "Maybe." A devilish glint in her greenish eyes, she glanced at B.J., who was fairly dancing across the tiles with curiosity, and added, "They can be an awful handful sometimes."

B.J. stuck out her tongue and gave Shannon a playful shove.

"But no date this weekend?" he asked, a shred of hope in his voice.

Shannon hesitated. It was tempting. But no, she couldn't, not until she was absolutely positive that Thad was just blowing smoke with his stupid threats. She'd been really firm with him that night.

Maybe that would do the trick. But until she knew for sure that Thad had given up, David Hamilton would have to wait.

Besides, this time she wanted to know a guy better before she actually dated him. She didn't want to make the same mistake she'd made before. Twice. Hadn't Thad seemed nice, too, once upon a time? And Charlie? Maybe David had all sorts of unpleasant habits. Like pushing unsuspecting by-standers into the pool at the club (she *hated* that); or throwing a tantrum when someone told him no; or telling three girls at the same time that he loved them. Things like that, that would make her hate him after she'd already learned to like him. She didn't want to hate him.

So she told him no.

There was a disappointed pause. Then, "Well, will I at least see you at the club tomorrow?"

"Sure." She did want to get to know him better. And the club was safe enough. Thad never went near there. "I'm on duty from noon to six."

He seemed to be taking her rejection of his invitation pretty well. That was a good sign. "See you there?"

"Sure, David," she said. "I'll see you there." No harm in that. She'd just said she'd "see" him.

She told him good-night and hung up. She was smiling.

"David?" B.J. asked with a grin. "You know someone named David? Is he cute?" Then, "Shannon's got a new boyfriend named David," she announced to Marilyn, who was scanning the contents of the refrigerator.

"I do *not!*" Shannon protested, alarmed. If B.J. ran around town blabbing to all of her friends what she'd just told Marilyn, Thad would hear it. She wasn't ready for that. Not yet. "That was just someone from the club, giving me my hours."

B.J. grinned again and tossed her long, straight brown hair. "Sure. And Marilyn's going to be Queen of this year's Sandcastles Ball."

"B.J.," Shannon said quietly, glaring at her sister, "I do *not* have a new boyfriend. And if you tell anyone that I do, your life will be a lot shorter than any insurance chart says it should be!" Then she added coldly, "And, Marilyn, you don't need another single thing to eat! You just had ice cream."

With that, she turned angrily and hurried out of the kitchen, leaving behind two startled younger sisters.

Chapter 8

Blaine had never seen any human being as relieved as Jeff Christian was when she told him she was tired and wanted to go home.

"Really?" The delight in his voice was unmistakable. He'd been fighting fatigue all evening. "Are you sure? I mean, you usually want to stay until the place closes."

Not tonight, Blaine thought without a trace of guilt. Tonight, the most fun would be after hours. She was meeting Duke on the beach, a date arranged while an unsuspecting Jeff was sitting alone at their table, eyes half closed. He'd thought she was in the women's room.

"You're not the only person in the world who gets tired, Jeff," Blaine said, picking up her clutch bag. "Watching tennis is a lot more tiring than playing it. Because it's boring!"

Jeff had no energy for an argument, so he let that pass.

On the way home, he took a stab at apologizing for "being such a drag." But he could tell Blaine wasn't listening. So he gave up, concentrating instead on the next day's match.

At 127 Hillcrest Drive, Jamie Smith was not, for once, thinking of tennis. Barefoot and wearing a short red-plaid nightshirt, she was standing in front of her dresser mirror wishing she had one of those little vanity tables with a cute matching bench or stool. Then she could sit comfortably while she tried to figure out what to do with that face and that hair for her date with Alex Krueger the next night.

"Girls like you," she scolded her reflection, "do not have cute little makeup tables with mirrors. That is the last thing in the world girls like you have."

She ran her hands through her short, straight hair. Little bits and pieces of it stood on end like the edges of a haystack. *"Urgh!"* she said through clenched teeth. It was hopeless. She turned in disgust and threw herself full-length across her bed.

Her room, she decided, was as plain as she was. No lace or ruffles, no gingham or calico, no dainty flowered wallpaper for this room. The walls were covered with tannish-beige grasscloth, the carpet was dark green, the furniture plain, sturdy dark pine. Trophies on shelves and framed certificates of athletic achievements on the walls were the only decorations. The room was remarkably clean and neat, testimony to Jamie's well-developed discipline. The credit for that went to her father's repeated lectures. "Neatness is a sign of order," was what he always said. "Order means discipline. An athlete cannot succeed without discipline."

So even if I'd failed at athletics, Jamie thought drily, my room would still be as neat as a furniture store's display window.

But I *would* like ruffles, she thought dreamily, rolling over onto her back. White eyelet ruffles, maybe. And tiny little flowers on the wall, and deep rose carpeting on the floor. And lots of green hanging plants. Then my room would look like a summer garden. That's what *I* would like.

But when her parents had decided to decorate it two years ago, Jamie had said simply, "Thanks. It's nice." She had never once mentioned ruffles.

Her new dress, bought that afternoon, was draped on a hanger stuck in the louvers of her closet door. She smiled. The dress, sleeveless and full-skirted, was white eyelet. And although it had no ruffles, there were tiny pink and blue flowers nestled closely together on the wide white belt. It was a pretty dress, a summer-night dress, a "real-girl" dress. Her mother would look surprised and say, "You went shopping alone?" as if Jamie were incapable of finding her way around a mall by herself. Just because she had never been interested in clothes before didn't mean she wasn't now.

Her father would probably ignore the dress and ask her if she had remembered to buy new tennis shoes.

Jamie giggled softly to herself. Maybe if she came downstairs tomorrow night wearing the new tennis shoes with the new dress, her father wouldn't even realize she wasn't wearing a tennis outfit.

No, she wouldn't wear the sneaks with this pretty dress. She would wear the white pumps, of course. Now, if only she could figure out how to magically transform her hair, so the dress wouldn't be wasted on her.

I should have bought a brown dress, she told the ceiling above her. Then I could have worn a grocery bag over my head and been totally coordinated, like the best-dressed people.

Groaning at the hopelessness of making herself pretty by the following night, Jamie buried the face she hated in a thick, fluffy pillow.

Blaine wasted no time returning to The Dunes to meet Duke. If Jeff noticed that her good-night kiss lacked its usual zing, he didn't make an issue of it. He had to be on the courts by nine the next morning. Murmuring a sleepy, "See you tomorrow," he drove away from the Hamilton mansion, hoping he wouldn't fall asleep at the wheel.

Blaine gave him a four-minute headstart. Then she jumped into her red Mercedes convertible and gunned the engine. Her parents were still at the club. When they got home and found her car gone, they'd assume she'd driven to the club earlier that night and met Jeff there. Better yet, they'd assume she was still with him. No questions would be asked at breakfast the next morning. She hated questions. They always demanded answers.

Duke was waiting for her behind the sand dune they'd chosen as a meeting place. The winds had shaped it into a mound resembling an old man with a long nose. Beach frequenters called it "The Grandpa Dune." The shape would change again and again over the summer, but for now the nickname fit. Blaine had picked it because it was directly beneath one of the tall, thin pole lamps that dotted the beach. Duke couldn't miss it. He'd be there.

He was. Struggling through the sand in high heels, Blaine called out a cheerful, "Hi! Been waiting long?"

"Thought you'd never get here," he grumbled as she gave up and slipped out of the sandals. "Where you been?"

They sat down in the sand in front of the dune that shielded them from the street. "I had to go home with my boyfriend," she explained. And then she lied. "He's very jealous. He'd have a fit if he knew I was meeting you." Jeff Christian was jealous of only one thing: someone else' s terrific backhand, but Duke didn't know that. If he knew she was less important than tennis or anything else to Jeff, maybe she'd seem less important to him. And that wasn't what she had in mind.

There was a noisy volleyball game going on at the eastern end of the beach, a bonfire surrounded by laughing people at the opposite end. The volleyball game held no interest for Blaine, but the bonfire looked romantic . . . and fun. She couldn't ask Duke to go with her, though, because someone there might know Jeff.

She settled in deeper against the mound. "So," she said, looking over at the thin guitar player, now in jeans and a white T-shirt, "what do you want to talk about?"

He laughed, a sound made deep in his throat. "If I wanted to talk," he said, "I'd go on the *Phil Donahue Show*." Duke reached for her.

Although Blaine surprised herself by thinking, I would rather be at the bonfire, she didn't argue. Summer was much too short to waste time arguing with the only interesting person at the club.

She only wished they weren't sitting quite so close to the overhead light. Suppose someone came along who recognized her? Blaine Hamilton in a musician's arms? Jeff would find out. And then she'd have no date for the Sandcastles Ball. She might be forced to go with some jerk who drove an old Chevy or Ford or worked in a supermarket after school. Yuk!

"This sand is scratching my skin," she said, pulling away from Duke's embrace. The ball was too important to risk for someone who wasn't going to hang around more than a few short weeks. She stood up and reached down to take his hand. "C'mon. Our cabana is just up the beach. It'll be more comfortable. And more private," she added coyly.

He jumped to his feet. "Well, all *right!*" He flung an arm around her shoulders as they began trudging through the sand. "With looks like yours, I didn't expect a brain, too. Unreal!"

Although he didn't know it, he had said exactly the right thing. It had been a long time since Jeff or any other boy had made a fuss over her. If she worked hard at being both pretty and smart, shouldn't a boyfriend notice? And shouldn't he say he'd noticed? Blaine banished all thoughts of Jeff from her mind and led Duke to her family's private cabana.

The next day was alternately cloudy and sunny, with a hint of rain in the air. Biking to the tennis courts at The Dunes, Jamie looked anxiously toward the blue-and-gray sky. Would the rain hold off until after the outdoor concert that night? The band shell was covered, but the audience, sitting on blankets on the lawn or in their own folding chairs, would be unprotected from the elements. The concert would be canceled if raindrops fell. If the concert wasn't on, would her date with Alex be off?

Don't rain, she ordered the scattered clouds above her. Do *not* rain tonight!

At the court, her father and Jeff were waiting for her. Her father was equipped with a video recorder. "I'm going to tape your match against Jeff this morning. Then he can come over to the house tonight and we'll watch the tape and pick out our mistakes."

"*Our* mistakes"? Jamie loved that. He meant *her* mistakes. They'd done this television bit before, several times. It never taught her anything about her game, because she could never focus on anything except the horrid way she looked. Was she the only one who noticed how perspiration shone on camera? The sheen of sweat on her face during a match was positively blinding! She hated those tapes. One day, she would confiscate them while her father was asleep or absent, and she would shred every single one of them into confetti. The only reason she had ever tolerated watching them was because at least, at *least* it brought Jeff Christian to her house.

"Can't," she said, removing her racket from its case. "Not tonight. I've got a date."

For the rest of Jamie's life, she would remember the stunned look on the faces of her father and the boy she had been in love with for years. Making that one simple statement, "I have a date," was more satisfying than any of her wins had been. If she said those words a thousand times again, they would never mean as much as they did that first time.

Her father recovered first. "A date?" he croaked.

Did shock give people laryngitis? "Yeah, you know," she said, grinning, "boy meets girl, boy asks girl out, girl says, 'Sure, I'd love to.' Like that."

"Who with?" Jeff asked, frowning.

Jamie had never had so much fun. The stands were beginning to fill with interested onlookers. How she wished they could hear the dialogue going on below them. "Shame on you, Jeff Christian," she scolded. "It's 'with whom,' not 'who with.' "

"Well, with whom, then?"

She loved the irritation in his voice. "With Alex Krueger."

"Krueger? That quiet kid? The brain? I didn't even know you knew him."

"I don't. That's what the date is for, Jeff." Her voice sounded so gentle, so patient. Like a nurse dealing with a cranky invalid. "The date is so we can get to know each other."

"Krueger?" her father echoed. "Never heard of him. Who's his coach?"

Jamie controlled a desperate need to laugh out loud. "He doesn't have a coach." She turned to walk onto the court, racket in hand, shoes carefully tied, sweatband in place on her forehead. "He doesn't play tennis," she added over her shoulder. "He doesn't even like it. Says it looks hot and tiring." She turned back to see what effect those words had had on her father, and wasn't disappointed. His jaw had fallen open and his eyes registered disbelief.

"It's okay, Daddy," she said sweetly. "It's just a date. If I decide to marry him, I promise I'll talk to you and Mom before I accept."

To Jeff, she said, "Can we get this show on the road, please? I have a lot to do today."

And she walked lightly, a bounce in her step, to take her place opposite the net.

Chapter 9

The closer Thad got to The Dunes, the more anxious he became. His palms on the steering wheel of his mother's sedan were so sweaty, his grip kept slipping. Losing his grip made the car swerve slightly on the dirt road leading to the hill above the beach. If he wasn't more careful, a policeman might stop him, thinking he'd been drinking.

His heart was pounding like the surf he hated.

Water wasn't supposed to roar like that. Water should be quiet and peaceful, like in a pond or a pool. The power of those waves crashing onto the shore terrified him. And the ocean itself was too deep and too dark. Who knew what kind of secret horrors the darkness held?

How could Shannon dive into those waters unafraid? Why had she taken this job? To spite him, he was sure of it. She had taken this job as beach lifeguard because she believed he would never come near there.

Well, she'd been wrong. His need to see her, to watch her, to know what she was doing and who she was with was even greater than his fear.

Not that he would actually set foot on the sand. He'd found a spot on the crest of the hill above the beach that was perfect. A cluster of thick bushes provided a screen, hiding him from those below him, and binoculars provided a clear view of the beach and the people on it. Especially Shannon. He could watch her all day and no one would know.

He pulled the car off the road, parking it behind a group of trees bent sideways by the wind. Then he got out and walked back to the bushes, where he settled down for the afternoon with fruit and sandwiches in a brown paper bag, a thermos filled with iced tea, and the binoculars.

Thus situated, he felt more content then he'd felt in a long time. A calmness settled over him as he lifted the glasses, focusing them directly on the white bathing suit and red hair in the tall white chair down on the beach. She hadn't escaped him after all, when she ran off to the beach.

Thad smiled thinly. It would be more fun if she knew he was up here. He wanted her to know she wasn't free of him here, in this place. But if she knew, she'd send someone to chase him away. That would ruin everything.

Maybe in his next letter to her, he'd hint that he was watching her. Yes, that sounded good. He wouldn't be giving away his position, but she'd realize that she wasn't safe at the beach, after all.

Had he said "safe"? Of course she was safe. He'd never hurt Shannon. He had meant . . . she wasn't "free" of him there, that's all. Thad began mentally composing the letter he would write Shannon later that day.

Below, on the beach, Shannon glanced around nervously. Her skin felt itchy. She couldn't shake the feeling that someone was watching her. Telling herself she was just being paranoid, she shook her head in an attempt to rid herself of her discomfort.

"You're shaking your head no," a voice called up to her, "and I haven't even asked you yet."

Shannon looked down. A smiling David Hamilton stood below, bare feet planted firmly in the sand.

"Asked me what?" she called. Funny — when he was around, the creepy feeling disappeared. She felt safer. Wasn't that silly, when she didn't really know him all that well?

It didn't *feel* silly. It felt . . . nice, like a warm sweater in winter, a cool dip in the ocean in summer. Nice.

"To be my date for the Sandcastles Ball. And don't say you don't know me well enough," he added hastily. "I told you all of my deepest, darkest secrets on the phone last night. You know more about me now than my parents do."

Shannon laughed. "You didn't tell me a single deep or dark secret. Except maybe that you hate spinach." She attempted to look disapproving. "Spinach is *very* good for you."

"If you'll go with me to the ball, I'll rush right out and buy ten pounds of spinach and eat every ounce of it."

Laughing, Shannon thought for a minute. The

ball was on Labor Day weekend, at the end of the month. Wouldn't Thad have given up by then? He couldn't spend his entire summer haunting her, could he? Nobody was *that* persistent. And she'd been really firm with him on the telephone the night before. Maybe he'd already given up. Maybe he was off somewhere looking for another girl right this very minute.

Besides, since when did Thad Wilcox tell her what to do? It was one thing to be careful not to deliberately anger him. But if she turned down this invitation from this perfectly nice person, she'd be handing Thad power that he really shouldn't have over her.

She had always wanted to go to the Sandcastles Ball. She had wondered if the chance to attend the big ball would ever be hers. And here it was, landing right in her lap.

"I'd love to go," she said.

David grinned up at her. "You mean it? You'll go with me? Great! Then how about going to the band concert in the park with me tonight?"

No. It was too soon. She needed time to make sure Thad really had given up on her. "Don't push your luck," she said, keeping her voice light. "I'm busy tonight. Now, go away! I have to concentrate on the water."

David put his hands up in mock self-defense. "Okay, okay! I'll settle for the ball for now. But I hate wasting all these balmy, romantic summer nights. I hope you won't be busy every night until the ball."

She wouldn't be. As soon as she knew for certain that Thad had taken her words seriously, she could begin dating anyone she chose. She would, of course, choose David.

"I won't be," she said calmly. "But I am tonight." If there was no sheet of yellow paper in the mailbox, no note on the kitchen counter in B.J.'s handwriting, saying "That jerk called again"; if Thad didn't jump out from behind a bush while she was on her way home, maybe then she could think seriously about going out with David one night the following week. "Call me later?"

"You bet!" If he wondered why she would be home when she had just said she was busy, he kept that question to himself. "Don't let anyone drown. See you later."

She watched him run down to the water and dive in. He was better at taking no for an answer than *some* people. A good sign. Especially since she doubted that he heard the word very often.

She was going to the biggest dance held by The Dunes with David Hamilton! Maybe her luck was changing.

She sat up straight in her chair. Daydreaming about the dance would have to wait. She had a job to do here.

But her skin was feeling itchy again. Shivering, she concentrated on the swimmers in the ocean stretching out endlesssly before her.

High above her, on the hill, Thad lowered his binoculars, his face twisted with rage. He'd been right to watch her! Who was that guy she'd been talking to? So blond, so tanned and healthy-looking, so sickeningly sure of himself. Thad's upper lip curled in a sneer. Did she really think she could dump him and find a new boyfriend on the beach, just like that?

Without Shannon in his life, he had nothing. Nothing!

It probably wasn't her fault, anyway. The guy had probably pushed himself on her. He looked like the type. The kind girls never said no to, the kind who never got dumped. His kind did the dumping.

And now he was moving in on Shannon. Thad's girl.

Thad raised the binoculars again. The guy was running across the sand to the water. He jumped in without hesitation, disappearing in seconds behind huge waves.

He'd have to keep an eye on the blond guy. If he made any more moves toward Shannon, he'd be sorry. She already had a boyfriend.

His tension easing now that Shannon was again alone, Thad resumed his self-appointed task. His legs were cramped, his face sunburned, and the salty sea breeze stung his eyes. But he had to stay and make sure that blond jerk didn't bother Shannon again.

Lauren, in denim cut-offs and a white T-shirt that spelled out in bright red letters, THIS SHIRT HAS NO MESSAGE, aimed the basketball and threw. It hit the metal rim, bounced once, and then dropped into and through the net with a satisfying swoosh. Her game of one-on-one with Rick on one of The Dunes' basketball courts was turning into a clear victory for her. She was ahead by six points. She couldn't believe it.

Neither, apparently, could Rick. Every time she made a basket, Rick would get a puzzled expression on his face, as if he had no idea how that had happened. After a while, Lauren found that annoying. Had he expected her *not* to be good? She'd already told him that she was the starting forward for the Varsity at Oceanview High. Did he think she'd won that position because of her looks? She'd won it because she consistently sent the ball into the basket where it belonged. Her aim, as Coach Dunne put it, was "phenomenal."

If Rick hadn't expected her to be any good, why had he asked her to play today?

Because he was sure he'd win, dimwit! a snide little voice answered. And here you are now, all sweaty, your hair all over your face, actually beating him. Gee, I bet he'll ask you out again in a hurry.

Right, Lauren thought dismally. When cows wear bikinis.

She didn't believe in deliberately losing to a boy in competition of any kind. Girls who did that were beneath contempt.

So why was it, then, that Lauren missed the next four shots? And two after that, until Rick was suddenly ahead?

She told herself her shots were off because she was rattled by his attitude. He had really seemed upset about losing. That had distracted her, so she'd missed a few shots. Simple as that.

Um-hmmm, the nasty little voice said. A few? If you missed that many in a row in a game at school, you'd be benched so fast your toes would curl!

"So," a happier Rick said as he expertly bounced the ball, "you want to go to that ball thing with me? The one on Labor Day weekend?"

"I'd love to," she said without hesitation, mentally sticking out her tongue at the nasty little voice. She was going to the best dance of the season with a *tall* person. She could wear high heels and she could tilt her head upward in that flirty way she'd seen other girls use, and she could lay her head on his shoulder without getting a cramp in her neck.

Excitement spurred her on to make the next eight baskets perfect shots. She beat Rick by two points.

But although he pouted a little, he didn't take back the invitation. They were still going together to the Sandcastles Ball, even if she *was* a female who wouldn't throw a game for a guy.

"You're pretty good," he said with some effort as they left the court. He grinned down at her. "You dance as well as you shoot hoops?"

"Yes," she said honestly, "I do."

"Great!" He took one of her hands in his. "It'll be a blast. I'm not too bad on the dance floor myself."

She decided he was right on target. Of course it

was going to be a great dance. She could hardly wait!

They passed Neal Winthrop on their way to the clubhouse. He had one twin firmly attached to each hand.

"Hi, Lauren," he said, smiling. "Rick. How's it going?"

"Great," Rick said, and they walked away.

As they left, one of the twins glanced backward and stuck his tongue out at her. Charming child. Obviously not overwhelmed by her natural beauty, charm, or wit. The question was, how did his older brother feel?

She told herself sharply, You are going to the Sandcastles Ball with a tall person, so what difference does it make how Neal Winthrop feels about you? Forget Neal. Concentrate on your date, Lauren Tolliver, or you might end up sitting at home with your cat on the night of the ball.

"So, Rick," she said deliberately, "tell me about the best game you ever played."

He was more than happy to do just that.

Blaine listened carefully that night at dinner as her brother described in glowing terms a girl he'd met. Blaine fought increasing irritation as he talked. She wanted to know who the girl *was*, not what she was like. Unable to stand the suspense any longer, she interrupted him in mid-sentence to ask rudely, "Well, what is this fascinating creature's name, David?" It had better be someone she knew.

It wasn't. "Shannon Murphy," he said happily.

"Murphy?" There was no one in their crowd by that name, Blaine was positive of that. "That's so . . . so uninteresting."

"Oh, for Pete's sake, Blaine," her brother said, annoyed, "get your mind out of the Social Register for once. Anyway, this isn't someone you're dating, it's someone I'm interested in. And I don't care about any of that snob stuff."

Blaine sniffed. "Just exactly where did you meet this Murphy person?"

"She's a lifeguard at the club."

"Lifeguard? You're dating a lifeguard?" Her voice was filled with horror.

Her mother laughed. "Darling, your brother didn't say 'murderer.' He said 'lifeguard.' I'm sure most of them are very nice people. If they weren't, they wouldn't be out there saving lives, would they?"

Blaine directed a fierce stare at her mother. "This isn't funny, Mother. A lifeguard at the club? Everyone will know! All of my friends will think my brother has lost his mind."

"I don't care what your friends think," David said, his voice matter-of-fact. "Most of your friends are certified jerks, anyway, except Jeff. If you had any sense, you wouldn't care what they thought, either." Then he excused himself, got up, and left the dining room.

This is not the end of this, Blaine thought. I'm not going to sit by and do nothing while my silly brother embarrasses the whole family with some ordinary little twit!

Chapter 10

Just before twilight, Alex, armed with a thick gray blanket, was waiting for Jamie at the white gazebo in the park where they'd agreed to meet. Neatly dressed in tan slacks and a pale blue knit shirt, he moved forward with a friendly smile to greet her. "You really look pretty," he said sincerely.

He meant it, that was the funny thing. Jamie decided it must be the dress and shoes. She hadn't been able to do a thing with her hair except shampoo the very life out of it and brush it back behind her ears. Ears she had firmly decided to have pierced first thing Monday. If they had to show (and with hair this short, how could she hide them?) they might at least be decorated. And since the only makeup she owned was a pale pink lip gloss, her face remained clean but bare, sticking out for all the world to see. Not that it was such a terrible face. But "pretty"? Hardly.

"Thanks. You look nice, too. Gee, it's really crowded, isn't it?"

It was. The earlier, threatening clouds had gone,

providing a clear and starry night for Oceanview music lovers. The ground closest to the bandstand was thick with bodies on blankets and chairs, leaving no vacant spots. That was fine with Jamie. Being surrounded by cymbals, tuba, and drum would make conversation impossible.

"Let's sit toward the back," Alex suggested, "so we can talk."

Jamie smiled. They were going to get along just fine.

Alex spread the gray blanket under a huge maple tree that served as their backrest. The music was rousing or soothing, depending upon the piece, the air soft and sweet, their conversation interesting. Darkness fell so softly, they never even noticed. When Alex reached over and took her hand, Jamie felt peaceful and content, a new feeling for her. It was an odd sensation, but one she welcomed. It was a little like the way she felt when she sat alone on the beach in the evening, watching the sun slide down behind the ocean, knowing that it would come back up again the next day. Contentment.

She settled back and relaxed.

Lauren practically had to drag Rick to the concert.

"Band music?" he had protested. "In the park? With ants and mosquitoes and wall-to-wall people? And they never have anything to eat at those things."

She'd bribed him by promising a pit stop in any restaurant of his choice following the concert. Food seemed to be tied with basketball for first place on Rick's Top Forty list. She'd never seen anyone eat the way he did. His leanness defied all laws of nature. By rights, he should have weighed three hundred pounds.

"You paying?" he asked in answer to her bribe.

Lauren sighed. "Yes, Rick, I'll pay." But she couldn't help thinking that she wouldn't have had to bribe Neal. He liked music.

Too late now. She was going with Rick. And the evening would probably cost her a bundle. She hoped the expense would be worth it.

It wasn't. The music was great, the night air soothing, their spot in the center of the park a good one. But two minutes into the second Sousa march, Rick, lying prone on the blanket Lauren had provided, fell sound asleep. And he snored. People around them pointed and giggled and Lauren had to force a smile, shrug, and pretend she didn't give a hoot, while irritation engulfed her.

Okay, Rick! she thought after a while, you lay there like a dummy, but I'm going to go get something to drink. A couple of enterprising kids had set up a lemonade stand at the edge of the park. Lauren got up and made her way through the crowd.

She groaned when she reached the makeshift stand, a card table covered with a plastic cloth. Standing in front of her, eager to relieve her of some of her money, were the twins Winthrop, Matt and Mart. Neal was nowhere in sight. He'd actually left these two alone? Unsupervised, they were probably preparing to practice highway robbery.

"How much for a glass of lemonade?" Lauren asked warily, fully prepared for any amount up to and including one hundred dollars.

"Twenty-five cents," came the surprising answer. "Lemons are very 'spensive, you know."

"I'll take two glasses." If Rick Van Winkle didn't wake up to drink his, she could always pour it on him.

"Hi, Lauren," a voice from behind her said.

When she turned, Neal smiled at her. So the twins hadn't been abandoned, after all. "Hi, Neal. Isn't the music great?"

He nodded. "You here with Rick?"

She resisted the urge to answer, "Sort of," saying instead, "Uh-hmm." No need to explain that her date wasn't exactly in the land of the living just now.

A serious expression on his face, Neal took her hand and led her through the darkness away from the lemonade stand. "Look, Lauren," he said when they were a safe distance from the two small boys, "I don't make a habit of stalking other guys' girls. So, are you and Rick a thing, or what?"

"Thing" seemed exactly the right sort of word. The question was, what sort of thing were they? It certainly wasn't the romance of the century.

"No," she said slowly, "I don't think we're a thing. I mean," she added awkwardly, "I don't really know him all that well." Knowing that a person liked basketball, rap music, and food didn't mean knowing them well, did it? The possibility that there wasn't any more to know about Rick crossed her mind. She brushed that awful thought aside very quickly, remembering that Rick was the person with whom she was going to be spending an entire evening on Labor Day weekend.

"Well, then," Neal said, looking up at her, "would you consider going to the Sandcastles Ball with me?"

It was amazing, Lauren decided, how quickly a person could gather her thoughts together when it was absolutely essential. Hers went like this: she would have a better time at that ball with Neal than she would with Rick, because Neal was more interesting. Rick fell asleep at concerts. Neal didn't, or he wouldn't be standing here talking to her now. And Rick wouldn't really care if she broke her date with him. She didn't bounce, couldn't be thrown through a hoop, and she wasn't edible. His disappointment would last no longer than, say, sixty seconds.

But, shallow or not, the vision of herself dancing in the big ballroom at The Dunes with someone taller than she remained steadfast in her mind. Just this one time, she told herself, just this once . . . and then I promise I'll become deeply intellectual and sensitive and considerate and thoughtful for the rest of my natural life.

Reading her mind, Neal said cheerfully, "I'll wear boots with my tux. I've got a pair with three-inch heels."

Ashamed that he'd read her thoughts, Lauren tried desperately not to do any mental adding. She failed. Five feet five inches plus three-inch heels equalled only five feet eight. He'd still be an inch shorter and that was only if she abandoned the idea of high heels. Hating herself, she said hastily, "It's not that. Really. It's just that Rick already asked me."

"Oh. And you said . . . ?"

"I said yes."

In the faint glow from the streetlight edging the park, she could see the disappointment in his eyes. Why did she feel like she'd just slapped him? She'd told the truth. Rick *had* asked her first.

But she hadn't told the whole truth. Which didn't matter, because she could see clearly that Neal had guessed it. He knew she wouldn't have gone with him even if she had no date. And he knew why.

To slide out from underneath the self-contempt that threatened to engulf her, she added, "But the club has lots of dances. Ask me again, okay?" After the Sandcastles Ball her newer, deeper self would say yes. That was, if he ever asked her again.

"Yeah, sure," he said without conviction, in the voice of a person who had just been rejected because of something he couldn't help.

Lauren felt like something washed in with the tide.

"Hey, are you gonna pay for this lemonade or what?" Matt yelled.

Neal laughed, breaking the tension. "They want their money. Mercenary little capitalists, aren't they?"

Lauren managed a laugh, too. They walked back to the lemonade stand. But Neal's eyes on the two cups of lemonade in her hands then seemed . . . sad, and the laugh died in her throat.

Impulsively, she said, "You'll be around tomorrow? At The Dunes?"

He nodded. "Oh, sure. See you there, right?"

"I'll be there. Maybe we can swim a few laps or something." She was trying to erase that look from his eyes. The one that said, I wish I was taller. Didn't she know what that felt like? How many times had she wished she were shorter? "Your brothers won't try to drown me, will they?"

He laughed.

Good. Very good.

"I'll protect you," he promised. "Enjoy the music."

He was such a nice guy. Too bad she wasn't as nice.

As she walked back to Rick, lemonade in hand, she salved her conscience with the thought that it wasn't all that nice to break dates, either, so maybe she wasn't such a terrible person. But, remembering the look on Neal's face, the thought wasn't much consolation.

Rick slept throught the entire concert. Lauren drank both cups of lemonade herself.

Jamie and Alex decided to walk to her house. It was his idea. "I'll leave my car here. It would take hours to get out of the parking lot, anyway, with all of these people leaving at the same time. I'll come back and get the car later."

He held her hand as they walked. Along the way,

they passed a store window, and Jamie caught a glimpse of their reflection. They looked very nice together. Tall, thin boy in glasses with a girl in a pretty white dress, short hair blowing slightly in the night breeze.

"So," Alex said, "tennis is your great love?"

She laughed, but it was not a happy laugh. "No. It's not. It's my father's great love. And my father didn't have a son to follow in his footsteps, so . . . I'm it."

"But you like it, right? You couldn't be that good if you didn't."

They stopped at the corner, waiting for the traffic light to change. "I used to like it. It was fun for a while. Then it . . . it just got hard. You were right. It's hot and sweaty and exhausting. That's all. Most of the time I feel like a wet noodle."

They crossed the street. He grinned over at her. "You don't look like a wet noodle." Then, "So, are you going to quit? Tennis? I mean, if you feel like that, maybe you should hang up your racket and try something else."

He made it sound so easy. "I think about that all the time. I just don't know how to tell my dad."

Alex frowned. "He wouldn't understand?"

Jamie laughed again. "Oh, sure. He'd probably say, 'Well, that's great, honey. What is it that you'd like to try next?' "

"You're being sarcastic."

"Yeah, I am. Listen, the only thing my father and I have in common is tennis. Without that, we wouldn't have two words to say to each other."

Alex thought about that. "What about your mom?"

"She knows tennis is all my dad and I have in common. So she goes along with it."

"You should talk to them. Tell them how you feel. Maybe they'd understand. Maybe they don't have any idea you feel that way."

Maybe they don't want to have any idea, Jamie thought. Aloud, she said, "You haven't met my father yet. He's not that easy to talk to, especially about something he doesn't want to hear."

"You have to try, though," Alex said quietly as they reached her street. "If you keep playing when you don't really want to, you'll get an ulcer or something." He grinned. "Maybe you'll wig out on the court, have a nervous breakdown."

Jamie laughed. He was so easy to talk to. She hoped her father had gone to bed. Maybe then she and Alex could sit out on the porch for a while and talk some more. It wasn't that late.

But when they arrived at her house, her father was firmly ensconced in the white wicker rocking chair, reading the Sunday paper under the porch light. She knew why he was there. He'd probably finished reading the paper hours ago, but he was determined to check out Jamie's date.

She wished with all her heart that she hadn't already told her father how Alex felt about tennis.

Chapter 11

Jamie's father hadn't been exactly wild about the idea of Jamie meeting her date at the park. "Afraid of meeting the old man, is he?" he'd asked.

She knew why he was upset. Because he was still hoping that one day Jeff Christian would suddenly look at her and say, "Jamie! How could I have been such a fool? It's you I love. It's always been you. I just didn't know it until now." And they would ride off into the sunset together, Jeff and Jamie, the Tennis Twins, a team that couldn't be beat.

That was her father's dream. And it had been hers, too. Until she met Alex. Now, she wasn't so sure. A life with Jeff wouldn't be any different from the life she led now, not until they were too old to lift their rackets. And then what? They'd sit around in rocking chairs, talking about nothing but the good old days? That didn't sound very exciting. Alex had so many interesting things to talk about. And he was a good listener, too, something Jeff wasn't . . . unless you were giving him tips on how to blast his opponent right off the court.

But even if *she* was ready to give up the Jeff-and-Jamie dream (and she couldn't be sure about that yet), she knew her father wasn't.

He'll ask Alex about tennis first, she told herself as she led her date up the steps.

"So," her father said when they'd been introduced, "Jamie tells me you're not a tennis buff. Ever tried the sport?"

"No, sir," Alex said politely.

"Ever going to?" Jamie's father stood up, newspaper in hand.

"No, sir. Probably not." Alex smiled. "It's a little too frantic for me. Swimming's more my speed."

Jamie's father waved a hand in dismissal. "Swimming is for fish. Maybe for a little fun now and then. For real athletes, there's nothing like the game of tennis."

"Daddy — "

"Can't imagine what you two have in common," her father went on, ignoring her. "Jamie eats, breathes, and sleeps tennis."

Now ask me if I like it, Jamie thought angrily. She willed her father to disappear. It worked. To her relief, he turned to leave.

"Don't stay out here very long," he warned. "You've got practice tomorrow, crack of dawn. And put a sweater on, so your arm doesn't get chilled."

Jamie clenched her teeth. If she started an argument now, he'd be out there all night. But she had no intention of draping a stupid sweater over her lovely dress. "Good night, Dad," she said pointedly.

"Good night. Don't forget what I said."

When he had closed the door, Alex said, "He's not exactly wild about me, is he? I mean, no chance of him starting up an Alex Krueger fan club, am I right?"

"Right. But it's not you. It's just that you don't play tennis. That's a felony in this family." Her voice was flat and tinged with bitterness.

After a moment of thoughtful silence, Alex looked down at her. "Does it matter to you? That he doesn't like me, I mean?"

She shook her head. "No. I told you, it isn't *you*. Don't worry about it."

Alex took a deep breath and let it out. "Then it's safe to ask you to the Sandcastles Ball? Will you go with me?"

Would she *go* with him? Did fish swim? Did birds fly? Was Alex Krueger standing awfully close to her?

"Yes," she said clearly, restraining herself with great effort from jumping up and down, "I will go with you." A ball! A real dance, with a very real, very nice boy.

"Great!" he said, and bent very quickly to kiss her good night. It happened too fast for her to react with more than a pleased smile.

"That is *some* smile," he said. "Now go in and go to bed. I don't want your father blaming me if you're dragging around on the courts tomorrow."

"Okay." She wished she'd been ready for that kiss. Maybe next time . . .

The thought that there would definitely be a next

time sent her floating upstairs. Cinderella was going to the ball. Now all she needed was a fairy god-mother to wave a magic wand and make her beautiful.

She dreamed that night of pumpkin coaches and glass slippers and a handsome prince.

The prince kept changing from Jeff to Alex and back to Jeff again.

Thad changed his mind about sending Shannon any more letters. She probably didn't read them, anyway. He would send her roses, instead: one single rose every day. Girls liked that kind of stuff. He should have done something like that in the beginning, instead of sending her those dumb letters. Sometimes his temper took over, making him do stupid things. It wasn't his fault. But now that he'd realized his mistake, Shannon would love him for sending the roses and take him back in a hurry.

He felt very important when he ordered the flowers. He was a man with a mission, and he was making progress. Soon Shannon would be his again. Then he could relax. But not until then.

When Shannon received the first rose — a single flower in a deep coral color, tied with a peach-colored ribbon but without a note, she assumed it had come from David. His way of reminding her about the ball?

She sniffed its fragrance, smiling. What a sweet thing to do! She'd have to remember to thank him when he called.

"Rose?" David said that night on the telephone. "What rose?"

Lauren and Neal had a picnic on the beach. She was dressed in a bright green jumpsuit, which looked great with her dark hair. Neal said so. She thanked him. She was having fun, and she was glad she'd accepted his invitation.

Then one of the twins ran up and shouted at the top of his lungs, "Hey, there, Jolly Green Giant!" Everyone within hearing distance found that incredibly funny. Lauren did not. She resisted the urge to dig a hole in the sand and bury herself.

When she went home later that day, she called Rick to invite him over for dinner. He *had* no younger brothers.

"My goodness," Lauren's mother said when Rick had gone home, "does he always eat like that? I've got to fix your father a sandwich now. He's starving. He says he came very close to grabbing that last pork chop before Rick got his fork into it. Your dad missed it by a hair, he said."

Lauren didn't find that funny, either. Nothing seemed the least bit funny these days. She wished the ball would hurry up and happen, so she could stop being shallow and concentrate on being a person with true depth, a person who didn't mind being laughed at on the beach, who didn't mind towering over a date like something leaning in Pisa.

Thank goodness, the ball was getting closer! She would just have to concentrate on being patient.

Wasn't that almost as good as having depth?

* * *

Shannon received a second single rose, this one as yellow as a canary.

On the third day, she waited on the front steps for the delivery van. "Don't bring me any more of these," she told the red-haired young man who ran up the walk, beribboned deep pink rose in hand.

"What?" He was young and eager and loved his work. He had expected to be greeted with a grateful welcome, not shot down in his tracks.

She firmly repeated her request.

"But they're all paid for," he stammered, thoroughly confused. He hadn't been warned about something like this. "My boss made me promise I wouldn't forget these singles, 'cause they're already paid for."

"I don't care. Your boss can give the money back. Just don't bring me any more of them. You can't force flowers on people who don't want them, for heaven's sake. Okay?"

"Not even this one?" He held out the long-stemmed flower.

She shook her red, wavy hair. "No. Thank you for delivering it. But please take it back."

Finally accepting that she meant what she said, he shrugged. "Okay, lady, if that's the way you want it." Turning away, he muttered, "But nobody ever turned down flowers before." Shaking his head, he took the rose back to the van and drove away.

Shannon went inside, convinced that there would be no more roses from Thad. But what would be *next?*

* * *

Thad, hiding behind a car parked across the street, witnessed the whole thing. Seeing it was one thing. Accepting what he'd seen took some doing. She had refused his rose! She had sent the man away without taking the rose from him. And he sensed, without having heard the words, that his order had just been canceled. He would probably receive a refund in the mail. The people at the florist's shop would know Shannon Murphy didn't want Thad Wilcox's roses. They'd probably joke about it because such a thing had never happened before. Everyone knew people never refuse flowers.

Clenching and unclenching his fists in rage, Thad moved out from behind the parked car.

"Hey!" a girl's voice called. "Hey, you!"

He looked up to see a red convertible sportscar, its top up, pulling up beside him. The driver was a pretty girl with white-blonde hair. And she was signaling to him. Still stiff with rage, he walked slowly toward the driver's side of the car.

"You calling me?"

Blaine Hamilton had been watching the same scenario unfold that Thad had. Finding the Murphys' address in the telephone book had been easy. They were the only Murphys in town. Ever since she'd heard from a friend that David was taking Shannon to the ball, she'd planned to do some detective work. Who would look after her brother if she didn't? This morning had seemed like the perfect time.

The yellow house was just about what she'd expected: geraniums on the porch railing, little white curtains at the windows instead of proper draperies, three bicycles lying on the lawn. No surprises there.

But the florist's van had been a surprise. And she had to admit that the girl in a short yellow dress who'd greeted the delivery boy was a real stunner. Great figure, long, tanned legs, all that red hair. But then, Hamiltons had good taste, at least in the looks department. David might not know class when he saw it, but he had a great eye for beauty.

But the redhead wasn't smiling and accepting the rose, the way a gracious person would. She looked like the delivery boy was there to burn down her house, not hand her something beautiful. And now the guy was turning, walking away, shaking his head, the rose still in his hand.

Maybe one wasn't enough for her. That would explain why she'd zeroed in on David. And poor David, the hopeless romantic, believed she loved him for himself, not the dozens of long-stemmed roses he could afford to send her. Silly boy.

Then Blaine noticed the pale, thin boy coming out from behind a parked car. His shoulders under a wrinkled plaid shirt were hunched, his head of dishwater-colored hair down, his body stiff and awkward. Could he have been hiding? He looked too old for that. Wasn't he about David's age? Why would he be hiding across the street from that girl's house?

He seemed to be on foot. Maybe he lived in the neighborhood. Which could mean that he might know something about Shannon Murphy.

She called out to him.

Her first thought when he stood beside her opened window, frowning in at her was, Wow, he looks mad! I wonder why. Hadn't he been watching the florist's van, too?

"Do you know the girl who lives in that yellow house?" she asked, leaning her head out the window slightly.

"Three girls live in that house," he said in a flat, hostile voice. "Which one are you asking about?"

"The redhead. The one who just went into the house. Shannon, isn't that her name?" Had this guy never heard of shampoo? Yuk!

He nodded. "Shannon's my girl," he said. He sounded both proud and angry, as if he were daring her to contradict him.

Shannon had dated *this* boy? Something about his eyes wasn't quite right. "What's your name?" she asked.

"Thad Wilcox. What's yours? And why are you asking questions about my girl?"

Something clicked into place in Blaine's head. "That was *your* rose she just sent back!" she exclaimed. "Why did she send it back?"

His face flushed an unbecoming red. "We just had a little fight, that's all. She'll get over it."

"Before the Sandcastles Ball at The Dunes?"

He eyed her suspiciously. "What about it?"

"My brother is taking your girlfriend to that dance."

"No! He can't!"

His vehemence surprised Blaine, even frightened her a little. This guy was really weird. Was she making a mistake by talking to him?

No. Who better to get help from than someone who was crazy about Shannon? "Well, he asked her. And she said yes. Are *you* going?"

He looked alarmed, his face going very white. "I never go near that place!" he cried. "I hate the ocean!"

Blaine laughed. "You live in Oceanview and you hate the sea? You poor thing! You must be the only person in town who feels that way."

"Yeah, that's me," he said more easily. He didn't want her to think he was a wimp. "The only guy in town who doesn't go to the beach every day."

"Look," Blaine said then, "I don't want them to go together any more than you do. If you think of some way to stop them, let me know. I'll help if I can. After all," she said smoothly, "you saw her first, right?"

Thad nodded.

"My name is Blaine Hamilton, by the way. Give me a call if you come up with something. I'm not wild about the idea of seeing the two of them together at the ball. It'll ruin my evening. See you!"

And giving him a casual wave, she drove away.

Thad was confused. How could Shannon be going to that dance with someone else? Hadn't she told him she wasn't seeing anyone? Had she lied?

He knew, suddenly, who the guy was. That blond guy on the beach the other day . . . his hair was almost the same color as this Blaine person's.

He had to do something. Because Shannon belonged to *him*.

Chapter 12

When Shannon's shift at the beach was finished one bright, muggy afternoon the following week, she met her mother at the mall. They went in search of the perfect gown for the Sandcastles Ball.

Shannon had never thought of herself as being particularly fussy about fashion. She liked simple, classic clothing and, of course, jeans. She was most comfortable in a bathing suit, but she could hardly wear that to a ball. That afternoon, nothing she tried on seemed the tiniest bit interesting. It had to be special, this gown.

After visits to half a dozen stores, Shannon was getting desperate.

So was Lauren. They ran into each other in a small boutique in the west wing of the mall. "Are you doing what I'm doing?" a ponytailed, jean-clad Lauren asked. "Stalking the stores for something stunning to wear to Sandcastles?"

"Yes. And I hope you're having better luck than I am. Than *we* are," pointing toward her mother at the front of the store, deep in conversation with the saleslady.

Lauren looked glum. "I'm not. They're all too short." Then she laughed. "Okay, okay, so I'm too tall. But you'd think there'd be a designer out there somewhere in the Junior fashion world who would make us minorities his or her mission in life. It's discrimination, that's what it is. I think I'll sue!"

Shannon laughed. "Have you tried The Tall Shop?"

Lauren made a gagging gesture. "One dress was actually metal-gray, if you can believe it. I would have looked like a flagpole! And another one was loaded, head to toe, with ruffles. I belong in ruffles like Eskimos belong in cut-offs."

Shannon didn't know Lauren very well, but she liked what she knew. Neal liked her, and Neal was nice. So Lauren must be nice, too. "Come on, I'll help you look. And you can do the same for me. And there's always my mom to give us her opinion." She grinned at Lauren, whose eyes were saying, You brought your *mom?* "It's okay. My mom is pretty neat."

They found Lauren's gown first, a pale sheath of some silken material. The fabric clung, accentuating Lauren's figure rather than her height. It was strapless, fitted at the bodice, and fell to the floor in clean lines. The dress rustled softly as Lauren walked back and forth across the thick carpet. The gown was completely devoid of ornamentation, and needed none.

"It's lovely, Lauren," Mrs. Murphy said. "You look perfectly beautiful."

Lauren flushed with pleasure. "Well, at least it's long. I can wear heels."

"Heels?" Shannon asked. "Won't that make you tower over Neal?"

Lauren's flush deepened. Shannon must have seen her swimming and talking with Neal at the club. "I'm not going with Neal. My date is Rick Leon."

"Oh. Well," Shannon said lamely, embarrassed by her mistake, "he's cute."

"Um-hmm. And he's . . . well, he's tall." Lauren had a feeling Shannon would understand that. Changing the subject, she said, "Now, let's find something for you. Who's your date, anyway?"

Shannon smiled. "David Hamilton."

Lauren's dark eyes widened. "Wow! No kidding? How long has this been going on?"

Having someone link her with David made Shannon nervous. Oceanview was a small town. Gossip traveled quickly. No more roses had been delivered, but she wasn't sure that meant anything. "I'm just going to the ball with him, Lauren. We haven't ordered monogrammed towels or picked out names for the kids yet."

Lauren looked properly chastened. "Sorry. Didn't mean to make you jumpy. I guess I have a big mouth."

"No, it's okay. You're not the one who's making me jumpy." Having delivered that mysterious statement, she said, "C'mon, you found your dress.

Now help me find mine. Something totally stunning, if you please."

They found it. Actually, Shannon's mother found it, to the relief of both girls hunting desperately through the racks. Mrs. Murphy's conversation with the saleslady had had a purpose. Just as Shannon was about to give up, the store employee emerged from a back room triumphantly holding high a plastic bag.

"This just came in," she said. "It's your size and I think it will be perfect on you."

It was. It was a beautiful shade of aqua, like the swirling sea on some days, and it reached Shannon's ankles.

"It's perfect!" Shannon cried, twirling around in front of the mirror.

"With that hair," the saleslady said, "you don't need a lot of color. This shade is exactly right for you."

Lauren grinned at Shannon. "Watch out," Lauren murmured, "when colors are *exactly* right for you, the price goes up."

Shannon laughed, and the girl in the mirror, lovely in aqua, laughed with her.

Lauren left the store first. She was meeting Neal at the club. They were going to swim for a while and then watch a tennis tournament. Unless, of course, the mini-monsters had blown up the courts while she was out shopping.

If it occurred to Lauren that she was more excited about spending the afternoon with Neal than she was about attending the ball with Rick, she quickly pushed the thought into her dress box and closed the lid.

Shannon, large maroon box in hand, decided to wait outside for her mother, who was paying for the dress. The little shop was stuffy and the two women would probably chat for more than a few minutes.

"Buy a new dress?" a voice said in her ear as she left the store.

"Thad! You scared me! Don't sneak up on people like that. You could give someone a heart attack."

"Someone would have to have a heart first," he said harshly, coming around to stand in front of her.

His appearance shocked her. He looked as if he'd been sleeping in the plaid shirt and baggy pants, and he needed a shave.

Shannon swallowed her guilt. It wasn't her fault! Other people suffered the same kind of rejection Thad had, and they didn't turn into zombies. What was wrong with Thad's parents, anyway? Couldn't they see what was happening to him?

"I know what that dress is for," he said slyly. "For that dance you're going to with that Hamilton guy."

How had he found out about that?

"You didn't think I'd find out, did you? I know everything about you, Shannon. You should remember that always."

His voice was low and harsh, his breath warm as he pushed his face close to hers. "You can't go with him," he hissed. "You're probably only going

110

with him because you think I won't go near that club. But I will, Shannon. You should have asked me. It's the ocean I don't like, not the clubhouse."

"Thad — "

"Quiet!" He pushed her back against the wall.

Where was her mother? Passersby ignored them. They probably thought Thad was just being romantic. The thought sickened her.

"You told me you weren't dating anyone," he said. "You lied!"

Shannon felt faint. Her head whirled as Thad pressed against her, his breath hot on her face. She couldn't breathe. She was going to pass out.

No, she wasn't! What was the matter with her, anyway? Thad wasn't that much stronger than her. He was just a person, for Pete's sake, and judging from the look of him, not a very healthy one. He looked like he hadn't had a good night's sleep or a decent meal in days.

She put one hand on his chest and pushed. Hard. She caught him by surprise and he stumbled backwards a few steps. "I didn't lie," she said. "And if you don't leave me alone, I'm going to call your parents. I mean it, Thad!"

The look he gave her then was a chilling mixture of disbelief and hatred. Was she being foolish not to be afraid of this person?

She had dropped the dress box when Thad pushed her against the wall. It lay on the brick floor between them. Thad bent and scooped it up before she could stop him, ripping off the lid, exposing the tissue-wrapped gown.

"Leave that alone!" Shannon cried. "Give it back! It's mine!" She reached out for it with both hands.

He ignored her, holding the box out of her reach. "Well, isn't *this* pretty!" he said with a sneer, lifting the dress out of its tissue wrap and holding it in one hand.

His hands might be dirty, Shannon thought dully. He'll ruin my beautiful gown. But if I try to grab it from him, it could rip.

"You don't deserve such a pretty dress," he said, his pale eyes fixed on her face. "Not if you intend to go to that dance with someone else." He dropped the box, taking the dress in both hands as if he were holding the wishbone from a Thanksgiving turkey.

He was about to divide her lovely gown into two separate pieces.

Maybe the dress would rip if she grabbed at it, but she'd rather have that happen in her hands, not his. She poised her body to leap at him.

"Thad!" Mrs. Murphy scolded as she came out of the boutique. "Be careful with that dress! It just cost me a fortune."

The transformation that came over Thad then was the most amazing thing Shannon had ever witnessed. His grip on the dress changed swiftly from a threatening one to that of a person displaying a garment, holding it carefully by its edges as if examining it. His body went lax, his eyes softened from wild to calm, and a thin smile made its way to his mouth. "Oh, hi, Mrs. Murphy," he said casually. "Shannon was just showing me her new dress. Great, isn't it?"

Shannon's mother looked from her pale, obviously shaken daughter to Thad, holding the gown gingerly now, as if he were genuinely afraid he might damage it. "Shannon? You okay? What's going on here?"

"Nothing, Mrs. Murphy," Thad answered calmly. He bent to pick up the box. Carefully replacing the gown, he said, "I guess Shannon was afraid I'd hurt her dress. Which I would never do, of course. But I can understand why she wouldn't want anyone handling it."

Shannon stared at him, her mouth open.

"Of course you wouldn't hurt it, Thad. I'm sure Shannon wasn't worried about that." To her daughter, Mrs. Murphy said, "Come on, hon. I've got a date. Tell Thad good-bye and grab your dress. Let's go."

Thad handed Shannon the box. "Have a good time at the dance," he said. But his cold, pale eyes sent Shannon a different message.

She shivered as she and her mother walked away. "He scares me," she confessed the moment they were out of Thad's hearing. "He's acting really weird."

"Well," her mother said, "you can't blame him for missing you." She put an arm around Shannon and gave her a quick hug. "You're pretty special." Then she added, "He seemed okay to me. That boy is *so* polite! Maybe you're imagining things. He seemed to have accepted the situation. I mean, he did tell you to have a good time at the ball."

Shannon gave up. She hadn't expected her

mother to understand, not after that Academy-Award-winning performance by Thad.

But she knew he wasn't giving up. She knew it as surely as she knew that no matter what Thad did, she was going to that ball with David Hamilton.

"Thanks for the dress, Mom," she said, putting the ugliness with Thad out of her mind. "I'll pay you back."

"This is true. Or maybe I'll just make it your birthday present."

Shannon grinned. "Mom. My birthday isn't until next April."

"So, I'll be early."

Laughing, Shannon gave her mother a hug, told her to go enjoy her dinner date, and went home to hang up her new gown.

Blaine was having trouble keeping her hours spent with Duke a secret. Her mother drove her crazy asking her why she looked so tired. So did David. "Burning the candle at both ends, Blaine?" he asked more than once. She told her mother she wasn't sleeping well. She told David to mind his own business.

Why wasn't he out with that Murphy girl, anyway? At first, she'd hoped that Thad Wilcox person had stolen Shannon back. But then David's tuxedo came, right on schedule. If Thad was going to do something, he'd better get moving.

Jeff was suspicious of her, too. It was all that yawning she was doing.

"Gee, Blaine," Jeff complained, "you make me

take you home early and then you act like you've been out all night! What's with you? I thought I was the party pooper."

She hadn't been out *all* night. She wasn't stupid. She didn't care how insistent Duke got, she had no intention of being totally foolish with him. Fun and games were fine. But that's all it was, and she wasn't giving up her whole future for some traveling musician who didn't even own a car of his own. For her own sake, she drew very strict limits on their fun and games. And so far, Duke had accepted those limits. He knew perfectly well who her parents were, and he didn't want to lose his job.

"I'm just sick of summer," she told Jeff as they danced at the club. That was a lie. Because when summer ended, Duke would leave and life would be boring again. "It's too hot and sticky."

"We could go swimming," he offered. "At the beach. It'd be fun at night. And it'd be something different. How about it?"

"No one goes swimming at night," she reminded him petulantly. "Not in the ocean. Anyway, the salt isn't good for my skin." She had no intention of going to Duke later that night with her hair dripping around her ears.

Jeff sighed. What was wrong with Blaine, anyway? If she didn't snap out of it before the Sandcastles Ball, that night would be about as grim as losing a major tournament.

He didn't see her smile as they passed the bandstand and her eyes met Duke's.

But Jamie Smith, sitting at a table with her parents, saw that smile and sat up very straight in her chair. What was Blaine up to now? That girl dragged trouble around with her like a puppy on a leash. If she hurts Jeff, she thought with vigor, I will personally wallop her with my famous backhand!

"Let's go home," Blaine told Jeff when the music ended. "I'm not very good company tonight."

Since that was an accurate statement, Jeff didn't argue. He took her home.

But she didn't stay there.

Thad sat on the unmade bed in his room at the top of the house, staring at the walls and their crazy-quilt patchwork of Shannon's image. She looked so sweet, so innocent in those pictures. Was she? Or had she tricked him? Was she really cruel and heartless?

He was so mixed up. He'd been riding a mental roller coaster all day. Visions of Shannon in that new dress flashed by him as he rode. She was smiling, laughing. But she wasn't smiling and laughing with him. That blond guy, the one on the beach, was with her. The one who had stolen her away from him.

How had that happened? He didn't understand. What had he done that was so wrong that Shannon wouldn't even talk to him? He'd done something bad, he knew that. But this time, he didn't know what it was.

And Shannon wouldn't tell him.

That wasn't fair of her. No wonder he'd been

angry about the dress. She'd told him a terrible lie. He'd asked her flat-out if she was dating someone else, and what had she said? She'd said no.

He stood up and walked to the mirror on his closet door. Twisting his face into a bitter smile, he said, mimicking a feminine voice, "Oh, no, Thad, I'm not dating anyone else, I'm too *busy!*"

He whirled, his face a mask of rage, and yanked one of the pictures off the wall. Taking it in both hands, he ripped it to shreds, letting the tiny pieces fall to the floor like confetti. Then, moving more quickly, he did the same to three more.

Suddenly, he stopped and groaned. His floor was carpeted with bits and pieces of Shannon's features, some in black-and-white, some in color: her nose, a piece of her chin, one eye, a thick cluster of red curls.

He sank to the floor. Maybe he could paste them together. He bent over the photographic jigsaw puzzle, fingering the pieces and muttering to himself about where he might have left his bottle of glue.

Shannon, at home watching television with B.J. and Marilyn, had no idea what was on the screen, because she kept seeing Thad's face at the mall that afternoon. He'd been so *angry*. She saw that face in the kitchen window while she was doing the dishes. And again in the bathroom mirror while she brushed her teeth. And in the glass on the front door when she went to turn on the porch light for her mother. She couldn't shake that image: Thad's eyes icy cold, his face full of fury.

The question was, where was Thad going to put all of that anger? Did anger like that just go away, disappear like a puff of smoke? And would it go away before the ball? And could she stop thinking about it?

She could. She would.

Forcing him out of her mind, she concentrated on the television screen.

In his room, Thad held the shredded photographs in his hands. He could never put them back together. They were Humpty-Dumpties. That's what his mother had called everything of hers he'd ever broken with his carelessness. "These are Humpty-Dumpties now," she'd say, displaying in her hands the shattered pieces of a vase or a lamp or some stupid glass doodad. "They cannot be fixed. No dinner for Thadeus tonight."

Even though he'd never broken anything on purpose.

He had to think. First things first. He had to remind Shannon that she belonged to him. And that she had betrayed him. That should be easy enough. Then he would forgive her, so they could always be together.

And he had to teach that blond guy a lesson, too. Show him that he couldn't just walk off with someone else's girl. That wasn't the right way to behave. He would have to be punished. The best way to do that was to snatch Shannon right out from under his nose, when he wasn't expecting it.

So they both wanted to go to that ball, did they?

Well, maybe he'd just let them do that. Yes, they could go to the stupid ball.

But they wouldn't go *home* together. He'd see to that.

Satisfied with his plans, Thad fell asleep on the floor, still clutching Shannon's shredded photographs in his hands.

Chapter 13

Jamie Smith was very disappointed by her mother's reaction to her announcement that she was going to the Sandcastles Ball.

"You *are?*" Open mouth, wide eyes, a long moment of silence. Then, "Well, isn't that something?"

Apparently realizing her mistake, her mother added then, "Who's taking you, hon?"

"Alex. The boy who took me to the band concert. Alex Krueger."

"I didn't meet him. Is he nice?"

Jamie nodded. She knew her mother saw her daughter as a plain sort of girl. The sort not likely to be asked to a ball. "Yes, he's very nice."

"Is he handsome?"

Jamie had to think about that. She saw Alex's face in her mind, the serious, intense expression on it, then the smile warming it, and the laughter in his eyes when she said something funny. She nodded. "Yeah, I think he is. I don't know whether you would or not."

Her parents always went to the ball. Was her

mother worried that she'd show up with a major social disaster and embarrass them to death? "I mean, his eyes aren't crossed and he has all of his front teeth."

Her mother laughed. "That's good. Well! I guess we'll need to go shopping for just the right dress, won't we?" She stared at Jamie.

Does she *have* to look at me like that? Jamie wondered. Like she can't think of a dress I'd look good in? "Don't worry, Mom," she said coldly, "I'll find something. Maybe I can find a dress with a hood and wear it backward." Adding, "See you later," she turned and hurried downstairs and out of the house.

She'd find her own dress! She was tired of her mother looking at her as if she couldn't figure out how such a pretty woman and handsome man could have given birth to such a plain child. Jamie didn't understand it, either. Her father was gorgeous in a stiff sort of way, and her mother had been Homecoming Queen in college. Where had she come from?

Perhaps because she was still feeling angry in the department store, Jamie bought a red dress for the ball. Very red. She loved it. It put color in her cheeks and even the saleslady's skeptical look didn't dampen her enthusiasm.

"Perhaps with a bit of makeup," the woman said dubiously. "But I do have a lovely peach dress that would be just wonderful on you, Jamie."

And I'll bet it's the plainest thing in the store, Jamie thought. I'll bet it isn't even really peach. It's probably peach-beige or peach-brown, like spoiled fruit. "No, thank you," she said firmly. "I'll take this one. It's exactly what I was looking for."

The dress, a crisp taffeta, nipped in tightly at Jamie's slender waist and then billowed into a short, bouffant skirt. It had a simple jewel neckline and pouffed short sleeves. "I could carry my purse in one of these sleeves," Jamie joked, knowing the saleslady wouldn't smile.

The saleslady didn't smile. "Are you sure about this, Jamie? It's very . . . red, isn't it?"

Jamie knew she meant sophisticated. Which I'm not, she thought. But maybe I could be, in this dress. "Charge it to my father," she ordered airily without even asking the price. If she could beat her brains out winning tennis championships for the man, the least he could do was buy this beautiful dress for her. "I'll take it with me."

Sighing, but unwilling to lose a sale, the woman obeyed.

And Jamie left the store with the world's reddest dress proudly tucked under her arm.

Shannon, trying hard to find reassurance in her mother's opinion that Thad meant her no harm, concentrated on forgetting about him and looking forward to the ball. That proved impossible when she began receiving roses again. But this time, they weren't delivered by a florist's van. They were thrust into the mailbox, one each day.

And every single one of them was dead. The leaves were crisp and lifeless, the bloom dry as paper, its color faded and dull.

"Gross!" B.J. fumed, tossing the dead flower into the kitchen wastebasket. "You *know* who's doing this, Shannon. Why don't you do something to stop him?"

"Like what?" Shannon asked wearily. She was relaxing in a chair at the table. It had been hot that day at the beach, the Winthrop twins had gone out too far twice, and people were being careless with litter again. She hated that. She was very, very tired, and not up to dealing with Thad or his stupid dead roses or her feisty sister.

"Call the police!"

"B.J., putting dead roses in mailboxes isn't a crime."

"Well, it should be!" B.J. slammed the cupboard doors as she unloaded the dishwasher. Her ponytail bounced angrily. "If I were you," she said emphatically, "I'd go straight to his parents. They should know what their darling son is up to!"

Shannon sighed. At least there hadn't been any more letters. That was something. How she had hated those yellow sheets of paper with thick black letters slashed across them.

"You should tell someone," B.J. insisted.

"I did. I told Mom."

"And?"

"And she didn't believe me," Shannon said flatly. "Thad pulled his Mister Manners act, and she bought it."

"I would never trust a boy who was that polite," B.J. said cynically. "Most boys have to work really hard at being polite. *That's* normal. And I'll bet you

123

didn't tell Mom everything," she added defensively.

"No, I guess I didn't. And don't you, either. It would just worry her. I can handle Thad." She said this with more bravado than she felt. He'd been so angry about the dress and the ball.

"Yeah? You and what army? He's losing it, Shannon, anyone can see that." B.J.'s voice softened. She looked at her older sister with worried brown eyes. "I'm scared he'll do something to you."

Seeing her sister frightened filled Shannon with fury. Thad had no right to do this to her and her family. No right at all!

"It'll be okay. He knows I'm dating someone else now, so I'm sure he'll forget about me. Quit worrying, okay?"

The person she really wanted to confide in was David. For one thing, it would explain to him why, although she'd accepted his invitation to the ball, she continued to refuse his offers to give her a ride home after work.

But she knew she wouldn't tell David. She couldn't bring herself to admit to him that she'd dated someone who had turned out to be so weird. He might understand. But what if he didn't? Anyway, Thad was her problem. And although she'd promised B.J. that she would talk to someone, right now she couldn't think of a single soul to tell.

Blaine knew exactly what everyone expected her to wear to the ball. Something black. Something black and strapless and very sexy. But she didn't intend to walk into the ballroom to a chorus of "Ho-hum, there's Blaine in black." A surprise would be much more fun.

It took more than one trip into the city, but she finally found what she wanted. It was pink-and-white peppermint-striped, in two pieces. Both pieces were made of a sheer, whispery gauzelike fabric, and lined in white cotton. The top was fitted like a short jacket, with long sleeves, a deep "V" neckline, and a high collar. The skirt was long and full, the peppermint stripes swaying as she moved about the showroom. It was the most innocent-looking dress she'd ever worn, and she knew that this pink-and-white peppermint-striped gown would get her far more attention than the sexiest black strapless gown in the world.

Jamie showed her new dress to no one, not even her mother. She wasn't ready for the look that would say, What was my daughter thinking of when she bought this flashy red dress?

She would show it to her later. Like . . . on the day of the ball, when it was too late to return the gown.

She hid the dress in its plastic bag in the farthest corner of her closet. Then she changed into shorts, T-shirt, and the new tennis shoes, and rode her bicycle over to The Dunes to practice. It was getting late, but the courts were well-lighted and they'd be uncrowded now. Most of the tennis players would be inside, dancing.

Including, she thought with a tiny pinprick of jealousy, Jeff and Blaine. Well, so what? *She* was going to the ball, too, in a dress that would catch everyone's eye. Blaine's would be black, of course. Something drop-dead sexy. Face it, Blaine would be sexy in burlap. Some girls were like that.

Jamie was leaning her bike against an equipment shed when she saw them. Two people standing at the far end of the shed, in the darkness. Blaine and . . . oh, great . . . Jeff! They were wrapped in each other's arms.

Jamie took an embarrassed step backward. The scene dug itself into her mind: two shadowy figures entwined, the bright blonde hair unmistakable even in the shadows, the sound of their murmuring . . . the intimacy between them, that, too, was unmistakable. Jamie was horrified. She was watching Blaine and Jeff in a very private moment. She backed away, scarcely breathing.

Then the shadowy Blaine moved aside for a second, and Jamie's breath caught in her throat.

Because the boy Blaine was wrapped around wasn't Jeff.

The guy was someone with sandy hair in a ponytail. Ponytail? The guitar player. The one she'd seen Blaine openly flirting with at one of the dances.

Blaine murmured something and laughed. The sound set Jamie's teeth on edge. If Jeff knew . . .

I could tell him, she thought, backing away on tiptoe until she could safely turn and run. He'd never speak to Blaine again.

No. He probably wouldn't believe me, Jamie thought as she reached a court, breathless. He knows I can't stand Blaine. He just doesn't know why. He'd think I was just acting mean.

And even if he did believe me, he'd hate me for telling him.

She picked up a ball and whomped it across the net. She wouldn't tell Jeff. He'd have to find out for himself.

Her conscience whispered to her, If you thought for one second that Jeff would turn to you when he dumped Blaine, you'd tell him so fast your words would trip over each other.

Jamie flushed with shame. This is true, she thought. But Jeff wouldn't turn to her. Oh, maybe for sympathy. But not for romance. He saw her only as a tennis buddy, nothing more.

Still, at least she had that.

What a wimp she was! No guts to tell her dad she was sick of tennis, and no guts to tell her good friend and tennis pal that his girlfriend had suddenly developed a deep and abiding interest in music.

Her forehand improved considerably that night as she walloped one ball after another across the net. Because each time, she told herself the ball was that treacherous Blaine Hamilton.

Her father-the-tennis-coach would have been impressed.

Chapter 14

Shannon received no more roses, dead or alive. There were no more letters and no surprise visits from Thad. B.J. assumed Shannon had talked to Thad's parents. Shannon let her think it. Now that it was all over, what difference did it make? She'd been right. By ignoring the problem, she'd made it go away. How wonderful it felt to be free of Thad! She was glad she hadn't confided in David. Now he'd never need to know about Thad.

"Tuxedo?" Mrs. Wilcox asked her son. "Thad, why on earth do you need a tuxedo?"

"For that big dance at The Dunes. I'm taking Shannon, of course."

"I thought you weren't seeing her anymore. You haven't mentioned her in a long time."

What was she talking about? He never told his parents anything about his private life. Never! And they were both too busy to ask. Now she was making it sound as if they made a practice of having cozy little chats. "Just give me the money, okay? If

I don't rent a tux today, there won't be any left in town. Everyone is going to this dance."

If she didn't give him the money, he'd take it out of her purse.

She gave him the money for the tux rental.

He remembered to say a polite "Thank you."

Jamie was having real difficulty dragging her weary body out of bed each morning. The end of summer was always the worst. So many tournaments, which she was expected to win.

And win she did. But it was much more difficult than anyone suspected. Playing in doubles tournaments with Jeff was the very worst, because she couldn't wipe out of her mind the sight of Blaine entangled with that guitar player. Every time she looked at Jeff, she lost her concentration. Losing her concentration meant that, sooner or later, she would lose a match. There was just no way around that. She felt like a time bomb ready to explode.

And she lost. A doubles tournament. With Jeff as her partner.

A shocked and disappointed "ooh" from the Oceanview spectators would haunt her sleep for a few nights to come. Their tennis princess had disappointed them.

She didn't care all that much. It wasn't as if this were the beginning of the Third World War. How important was the loss of a doubles match, anyway?

Very, according to Jeff Christian. Once the shock had worn off, he was furious. "No wonder we lost!" he raved as they left the court. "You played like a two-year-old! Where was your head, anyway?"

Jamie had never been so tired. Her head ached. Her knees felt like melted butter. And she still had to face her father.

But she was not going to take all the blame for this loss. The term used here was "doubles", as in two people. She hadn't been playing all by herself. And Jeff hadn't performed much better than she had.

She whirled to face him. "Look who's talking! And where exactly was *your* head? You weren't concentrating, either. I suppose you were thinking about Blaine and her new boyfriend — that stupid guitar player!"

The stricken look on Jeff's face cut off her words as effectively as if he'd used a knife on them.

She drew in her breath. "Oh, Jeff, I'm sorry. I mean . . . I didn't mean anything, honest!" Well, that wasn't true, but she couldn't stand the shock on his face. Or *was* it shock? He looked more hurt than shocked. Chances were, he'd already suspected something, and she'd simply confirmed it. But a person would hate having that kind of suspicion confirmed, wouldn't he? "Forget it, please," she begged. "Just forget I said that. It was stupid."

Without a word, Jeff whirled and rushed off toward the locker room.

Jamie sagged against a wall. She'd had enough for today. All she wanted to do now was slither home and bury herself in her bed.

No such luck, she thought in misery as her father railed about her game all the way home. He said he couldn't believe they'd lost the doubles trophy. He said he hadn't seen such sloppy playing since she was eight years old. He said Jeff would probably never forgive her.

So, when they got home, she faced him in the kitchen and said, "And you, Daddy? How about you? Will *you* forgive me for losing today?" She tasted salt on her lips and was surprised to discover that tears were quietly falling from her eyes. Her father hated tears. He always said they served no useful purpose. Well, without winning at tennis, neither did she.

"Your father isn't angry with you, Jamie," her mother said. "He's just upset."

"Oh, he is *so* angry!" Jamie burst out. She stood facing her father. "You just can't handle this, can you? I embarrassed you in front of the whole town!" Lowering her voice, swiping at her sweat-and-tear-streaked face with the back of her hand, she said, "I always knew you only loved me because I was good at tennis. You could brag about that as long as I kept winning. Well, now I've lost, so you don't have to love me anymore."

"Jamie!" There was shock and horror in her mother's gasp.

"And I'm *not* playing tennis," Jamie continued, "not ever again! I'm sick to death of that stupid game!"

When her father, too shocked to speak, remained silent, Jamie shouted, "I'm a *girl*, Daddy! I'm not your son, I'm your *daughter!* And that's what I want to be. I want to act like a girl, have the kind of fun other girls have. If you can't hack that, it's too bad." She was sobbing openly now, her emotions completely out of control. "I *hate* this thing!" she cried, and lifted her racket and hurled it. It hit the kitchen table with a sharp whack. But the sheer force behind her powerful arm sent the racket ricochetting off the table and slamming into her father's left knee.

When he cried out in surprised pain, Jamie uttered a low moan. She turned and ran out of the room, up the stairs to her bedroom, where she threw herself across the bed and sobbed her heart out.

Jeff, showered and calmer now, went straight to Blaine. She was sitting poolside, lounging in a yellow bikini.

"Hi, sweetie!" she said nonchalantly, extending a bottle of suntan oil. "You're just in time to do my back."

"I don't want to do your back," he said coolly.

Frowning, Blaine sat up straight. She had already heard that he'd lost the doubles trophy. Was that his problem? It wasn't like him to be rude.

"I want to know what's going on with you and that guitar player."

Blaine wasn't really all that surprised. It was hard to keep any secrets in their little town. She thought fast. Jeff had never been angry with her before, so she wasn't sure which way to go with this. Tell the truth and beg forgiveness? Yuk! Begging sounded so . . . common. And telling him about Duke would practically be the same thing as telling her parents. Their daughter involved with a traveling musician? She'd be packed off to private school in some bizarre place like Outer Mongolia.

No. Confession might be good for the soul, but in this case it would definitely kill her social life. Duke couldn't escort her to the ball. So her escort had to be Jeff.

"*What* guitar player?" she asked innocently.

When the knock came on Jamie's bedroom door, she was sure it was her father.

"Come in," she said wearily, sitting up on the bed.

The person who came in wasn't her father-the-tennis-coach. It was her mother-the-Homecoming Queen. She was carrying a red velvet case and a large paper bag. "Makeup in this one," she said, moving into the room and holding up the red case. "Hot rollers, curling iron, cream rinse, and mousse in this one," dropping the paper bag on the bed. "Maybe this isn't the best time to see what a pretty girl you are, with your eyes all swollen like that. But I thought of that, too." She opened one hand. In it were two limp, wet teabags. "Lie down and put these over your eyes while I check out your dress. You *did* find a dress, didn't you?"

Jamie closed her eyes and applied the soggy tea bags. They felt cool and comforting. She didn't want her mother to see the dress. Because she knew it was all wrong. She'd known it almost since the first day she'd brought it home, but couldn't admit it until now. She'd been trying to prove something by buying that dress. All she'd proved was that she was a total jerk! "It's in the closet," she murmured. "Plastic bag, way at the back."

She heard the zipper slide down and held her breath.

"Who sold you this?" her mother said quietly, after a long moment of silence.

"Nettie. At Frillz 'n' Fancies. But it wasn't her fault, Mom. I wouldn't let her talk me out of it. And believe me, she tried!" Tears stung her eyelids again, defeating the purpose of the tea bags. "It's an awful dress, isn't it?"

"No, it isn't. It's really very pretty."

"It is?"

"Sure, honey. But taffeta is too hot for August. And red is just not a summer color. This must have been part of Nettie's fall collection."

"Do I have to take it back?" Nettie wouldn't be smug and say I told you so. She was nicer than that. Still . . .

"How about if we just put it back in your closet until Christmas? This would be just perfect for a holiday dance."

Jamie felt such a rush of love for her mother, it took her breath away. Because two things had just been said: that her taste in clothing wasn't atrocious, after all, and that her mother believed she would be invited to a Christmas dance.

"Oh, wow," she said softly. "Thanks, Mom."

Then, "But what'll I do about a dress for Sandcastles?"

"Just wait one minute. I'll be right back."

When her mother returned, she told Jamie to sit up and remove the tea bags. "Well," she asked when that had been accomplished, "what do you think?" She was holding in front of her a long gown on a hanger.

The dress was beautiful. And the really strange thing was, it was peach. Nettie had had the right idea all along. And this dress wasn't peach-beige or peach-brown. It had dainty peach flowers on a white background — an old-fashioned kind of gown, with long, sheer sleeves trimmed with delicate lace at the narrow cuffs and a high lace collar. Tiny white buttons decorated the bodice. The skirt, over a ruffled petticoat, flowed softly from the waist. It reminded Jamie of the way she would really prefer to have her room decorated.

"I haven't worn it yet," her mother said as Jamie stared in delight. "It should fit you. I can always take it in here and there if necessary."

"You were going to wear it to the ball yourself, weren't you?" Jamie said, her voice full of awe. Her mother thought her daughter could do justice to this beautiful dress? This beautiful gown that a Homecoming Queen had planned to wear?

"Oh, honey," her mother said with a gentle laugh, "I've got at least five gowns in my closet. I can wear any one of them. Now, come into the bathroom with me so I can work my magic."

Jamie got up and obeyed, feeling as if she'd fallen

asleep and was deep in the middle of a wonderful dream. But the heat from the curling iron a few minutes later was very real.

She never would have believed that it would be her own mother acting the part of the fairy godmother.

"We should have done this a long time ago," her mother said, trying doggedly to wind the shortest of hair around the hot iron's barrel. "I guess I told myself you liked things just the way they were because that made it easier for me. I'm sorry, Jamie. And your dad is, too."

"He'll hate me."

"He won't hate you. He loves you very much. He just has to realize that you're *you*. And that you're growing up. You have to help him see that. Now hold still, so I can get this one . . . last . . . strand. There!"

Her hair looked cute. Not gorgeous or sexy or sophisticated, but cute, curling softly around her face like that. "I can't believe you got this stuff on my head to curl," she said with admiration.

Her mother laughed. "Magic, honey, just magic. Nothing to it. Pay attention now, so you can do this by yourself the next time." And she set to work with eye shadow, mascara, eyelash curler, blusher, and lip gloss.

It took only fifteen minutes to transform an astonished Jamie.

"You had it all along," her mother said as Jamie stared in wonder at her reflection in the bathroom mirror. She looked one hundred percent pretty! No question about it. "You just didn't know it. Now, why don't you go downstairs and show your father that you've grown up?"

The look in her father's eyes when Jamie walked into the living room told her her mother had been right. He honestly hadn't realized that she was no longer the five-year-old willing to hoist a heavy tennis racket just to please Daddy.

"You look . . . beautiful," he said softly, standing up as she came hesitantly into the room. "Like your mom when I first met her. In high school."

"Oh, Daddy, I'm wearing grungy old shorts and a T-shirt. I can't look beautiful in this!" But she was pleased. Because she knew he meant it.

"Yes," he said firmly, "you can and you do."

There was an awkward pause then until he said, "Look, Jamie, I'm sorry. I pushed you into something *I* wanted, and I never asked you how you felt about it. I thought you liked tennis. But that's no excuse," he added hastily.

It wasn't all his fault, she realized now. She should have told him how she felt. Alex had been right. She shouldn't have expected her father to guess her feelings. And she should have had the courage to tell him herself. "I did like tennis. I do." And she knew that she still did. "I just don't want it to be my whole life anymore, okay? I want what other girls have, what Mom had when she was my age." She smiled at him. "I'm not sorry I learned to play tennis well, Daddy. Everybody needs something they can do well. But now I need to learn how to do other things, too."

She was astonished then, to see what looked like tears in her father's eyes. Well, he wasn't really crying. The tears were just sort of sitting on his eyelids, as if they were waiting to see what happened next. Her macho father . . . this day was just full of surprises.

"Earlier, there," he said haltingly, "it sounded like you sort of hated me."

"Oh, Daddy, of course I don't hate you! I could never hate you. And I *will* play in the singles tournament tomorrow." She grinned. "But I'm not stepping one foot outside of this house without makeup or mousse."

He tried, and failed, to return the grin.

It's going to take a while, she thought sadly. He's not going to get over this in five minutes. But she couldn't take back what she'd said because she'd meant it. Most of it.

"You're all grown up," he said then. "And I didn't even notice. I'm sorry."

"It's okay, Dad. Honest! And I'm *not* all grown up. Not yet. I could still use an expert bear hug every once in a while, for instance. Like . . . well, like right now."

And if the bear hug he gave her then wasn't quite the same, well, that was okay, too. It would have to be. Because whichever direction she went in now, it wasn't going to be backward.

Chapter 15

Jamie won the next day, retaining her Junior Singles Championship title. But that was nothing compared to the thrill of stunning Jeff when she first danced out onto the court wearing what she called her "new face."

"Jeff, you're staring," she pointed out with glee.

"I'm sorry," he stammered. "But you sure look great!"

The surprise in his voice annoyed her a little. He made it sound like an event, like the invention of the wheel. Had she been so unattractive before this transformation?

When she walked off the court to receive her trophy, Jeff was right there, towel in hand. "Boy, you looked terrific out there! Congratulations!"

He meant her playing looked great, didn't he? Or did he? He couldn't seem to take his eyes off her, and hovered nearby while photographers snapped her picture and reporters asked her the same old questions.

When all of that was finished, he walked her to

the locker room. "Listen," he said before she went inside, "maybe we could do something else together besides play tennis."

Jamie hid a grin. All it took was a little makeup and a curling iron. Was Jeff that shallow? "Like what?"

Jeff hesitated. He already had a date for Sandcastles. But Blaine's story about the guitar player (that he was a friend of her father's) was a hoot. Like Harper Hamilton had pals with ponytails! Did Blaine really think Jeff Christian was that stupid?

Impulsively, he answered, "Like the Sandcastles Ball. We could go to that together." He'd deal with Blaine later. Going with someone else would show her how much he hated being lied to.

He's furious about that guitar player, Jamie told herself. Had he broken his date with Blaine? Or is he planning to do that later, if I say yes now?

She had dreamed of a moment like this for so long. But never once in her dreams had she already had a date with someone else when Jeff asked her out.

"I can't," she said with some regret. "I already have a date."

Did he have to look so surprised? "With Alex Krueger," she added coolly. Alex and David went to the same high school, although she knew they didn't hang out with the same crowd.

"Krueger? Oh. Nice guy."

"Yes. Very."

He was frowning, as if he couldn't figure out how things had turned around on him: first Blaine and that musician, now Jamie and Krueger. "Well, maybe you could save me a few dances," he added as she turned to leave.

"Sure. Why not? See you there!" She practically waltzed into the locker room. She was going to dance with Jeff! She could hardly wait for the ball. Labor Day weekend, hurry up!

Happier than she had ever been, Jamie sang in the shower.

By the time Labor Day weekend did arrive, two of the girls attending the ball were falling in love. Both were unhappy about it. Lauren Tolliver was unhappy because the object of her affections was *not* her date for the ball. She was falling in love in a big way with Neal Winthrop, more so each time she saw him, yet she was going to the last big dance until Christmas with Rick Leon, who was about as interesting as stale bread. True, she didn't *hate* Rick. But on a scale of one to ten, Neal was a definite eleven (even with points off for lack of stature), while Rick was no more than a paltry four or five. Maybe a six, because he *was* cute. But what girl in her right mind would choose a six over an eleven?

A shallow one, Lauren scolded her mirror image as she dressed for the ball. This was your choice, Lauren Marie Tolliver, so quit whining!

She had decided to let her thick, dark hair hang loose in waves. Many of the other girls would have elaborate upswept hairdos, but that would add an extra inch or two to her height. She had a lot of hair.

Neal would be at the dance. He was going stag. But he probably wouldn't ask her to dance, since he knew why she was going to this ball with Rick instead of with him.

And if he didn't ask her to dance, she had only herself to blame. A rotten thought to begin the evening with. But true. She'd just have to live with it.

Shannon Murphy was falling in love, too. With David Hamilton. She had fought against it. She'd made two mistakes, back-to-back, and she'd paid for one of them right up until very recently. Thad had finally given up, but the ugliness was hard to shake. She didn't ever want to go through anything like that again!

Of course, David wasn't anything like Thad. She and Thad had seldom laughed. She and David laughed all the time. And now that she was no longer afraid of Thad, she was finding it almost impossible to resist David's warmth.

Shannon slipped the aqua dress over her head. B.J. zipped it up the back for her.

"Oh, Shannon," she whispered, "you look so beautiful!"

Marilyn, sitting on Shannon's bed, was not so easily impressed. "How come you didn't buy green?" she complained, casting a critical eye on Shannon's flowing aqua-colored gown. "Green is prettier than blue."

"It's not blue, dummy!" B.J. said. "It's aqua! Like the sea!"

B.J. shrugged. "So how are you going to wear your hair? Up or down?"

"Half-and-half. The sides clipped up, the back loose." Would David like that?

The doorbell rang. "I'll get it!" Marilyn cried, and ran from the room. She came back several minutes later, frowning. "You got *two* corsages," she said. "How come he sent you two?"

Shannon took the small plastic boxes from her sister. Both contained orchids. She lifted the lid from the first box and read the tiny card inside. *Thanks for saying yes. Love, David*, she read.

The second card was blank. Her skin suddenly felt cold and clammy. She shook the feeling away, determined not to spoil the evening with some silly, unfounded fear. "The florist must have made a mistake," she said, laying the boxes on her bed.

"Maybe David likes you so much that he sent you two corsages," Marilyn suggested. "Tommy Morrison said David is really rich. He said the Hamiltons live in a mansion. Are you going to the ball in a limousine?"

"No." Shannon shook her head. "We think they're silly. We're going in David's car." She didn't add that David's car was a Jaguar. She didn't want her sisters to think his money was important, because it wasn't. She knew now that if his father lost every penny of their money the next day, she would still be in love with David. He had been so patient, waiting until she'd been sure Thad had given up. Only then had she accepted David's offer of a ride home after work. Only then had they had some time alone.

She ran a hand across her lips dreamily, remembering his good-night kiss. It would stay with her forever. Because he had meant it.

And so had she.

"C'mon," she said, snapping out of her daydream. "Help me with this choker." It was made of pearls, which reminded Shannon of the sea.

"Aren't you going to wear any earrings?" a disappointed Marilyn asked. She had already picked out a pair she thought especially pretty.

"No. This dress doesn't need it." Now, if only she could relax, have a good time, and forget that she wasn't supposed to be falling in love with anyone because it was probably a big mistake. If she could do all of that, she just might have a good time.

But what if the florist *hadn't* made a mistake? What if Thad had sent that second corsage as some sort of message?

Shaking off that scary thought, Shannon picked up a lightweight crocheted shoulder wrap, and left the room.

Thad adjusted his cummerbund and wondered if Shannon had received the corsage yet. He knew David Hamilton had probably sent her exactly the same flower. Rich guys always sent orchids.

He wasn't going to her house. He wanted her to go to the dance with Hamilton, he'd decided. Because he wanted the guy there when he took Shannon away. Maybe that would show him what it felt like to have someone stolen from you.

When he came downstairs, his mother stared at him. He thought it was because he looked so great in the white tuxedo with the red cummerbund. A red carnation decorated the lapel of his jacket. He thought it made a nice touch.

Then she said slowly, "Thad? Thadeus, you can't go like that!"

He looked down at his tux. It was perfect. "Why not?"

She got up and came over to stand in front of him. Tall, elegant, every hair in place. Like a mannequin in a store window. "Your hair," she said, "you haven't washed it." She frowned. "Not for some time, apparently. It isn't even combed properly." She looked down at his hands. "And your nails are filthy. Oh, really, Thad, what's come over you? You know better than that!"

It was true. He did. Once, when he was little, he'd come to the dinner table after an afternoon of play, with dirty hands. They'd had company that night — his father's boss and his wife, people his mother was trying to impress. When their guests had gone, his mother had locked him in the bathroom for what seemed like hours.

He had never come to the table again with so much as a smudge on a finger.

And he had never looked at his mother in quite the same way again.

But he wasn't little anymore. She couldn't tell

him what to do. And he'd like to see her try to lock him in. He was three inches taller than her, and a lot stronger.

"Don't worry about it, Mother" he said coldly, brushing past her. "Shannon loves me for myself, not for the way I look!" And he pushed the front door open.

"Thadeus!"

He ignored her and kept on going.

Blaine was extremely satisfied with the way she looked in the peppermint-striped gown. It provided exactly the effect she wanted. With her hair piled softly on top of her head, a wreath of tiny pink roses and white baby's breath encircling the cluster of curls, the look she'd achieved was one of sexy innocence, if there was such a thing.

Jeff would love it. He had never liked the slinky gowns she usually wore. And Duke, well, Duke would just give her that cynical grin of his. Meaning, Who do you think you're kidding, Blaine?

She just hoped people took the time to look at her feet. Having peppermint-striped shoes custom-made had been a real headache. Her father would have a fit when he saw the bill.

But why dress up if you weren't going to do it right?

The grandfather clock in the upstairs hall struck eight o'clock. Blaine smiled with satisfaction. Jeff would be here with the limo any minute now. It was time for the Sandcastles Ball.

She was ready.

Chapter 16

The look on Alex's face when Jamie came downstairs in the peach-flowered gown warmed her from
her head to her toes. It was similar to the look on
her father's face, although Alex's was not the least
bit parental. Seeing the warmth and admiration for
her in their faces, Jamie felt very loved and appre-
ciated. For something that had nothing to do with
her backhand.

"You look beautiful," Alex said softly, handing
her a large white box and an even larger smile.

"Thank you. So do you." And he did, in a white
tuxedo and matching cummerbund. His boutonniere
was peach. Her own corsage was miniature peach
rosebuds. He must have called her mother to ask
about her dress. But instead of asking Alex to pin
on the corsage, she turned to her father, who looked
splendid in a black tuxedo. "Dad?" She handed him
the box. "Could you pin these on me, please?" Alex
would understand. She had told him about her big
blow-up and its resolution.

Her father smiled. "Sure, honey." Doing the honors, he said, "You're going to be the prettiest girl there."

Well, of course she wasn't. But she'd waited a long time to hear her father say she was pretty and she wasn't going to argue with him now. "Thank you. You look pretty good yourself."

Her mother, lovely in a pink strapless gown with a waist-length, long-sleeved jacket, smiled at both of them.

"Ready?" Alex asked when the corsage was fastened securely.

"Ready." Jamie smiled. Hadn't she been ready for this all of her life?

They left for the ball.

Shannon had been in the ballroom several times since she'd started working at The Dunes. A huge, high-ceilinged rectangular space with white walls and long, narrow windows, it hadn't impressed her. The smaller Surf Room was much cozier and prettier.

But she drew in her breath in delight when she and David stepped through the wide doorway. The ballroom had been transformed into a warm and welcoming fairyland of candles and lights.

At first, Shannon thought they had somehow removed the ceiling, exposing the dark sky full of stars. Then she realized that the stars were really hundreds of tiny clear lights. Other lighting came from a giant crystal chandelier hanging over the center of the room and matching wall sconces, all holding flaming candles that cast a glow over the room. Each small round table, situated around the edges of the ballroom and covered with a sea-green floor-length cloth, held in its center a miniature ceramic sandcastle, complete with turrets and towers that served as more candleholders. Tall palm trees in pots were grouped in the room's four corners, their trunks completely covered with additional strings of the tiny clear lights.

"Are those palm trees real?" she whispered to David. She had no idea why she was whispering. Perhaps it was because the intimate, softly lit setting seemed to call for whispering.

"Yep," he answered. "My mother's idea. They'll be planted near the beach later."

"What a neat idea! And everything looks so beautiful!" She turned and pressed her face against his chest. "Oh, David," she murmured, "we're going to have such a wonderful time." Afraid she might get makeup on his white tuxedo, she lifted her head. "Did your mother do all this?"

He laughed. "No, she did what she usually does. She hired someone. She just gave the orders. I'm glad you like it."

They had been among the first arrivals. But the ballroom was quickly filling up with guests both young and not so young. Unlike high school dances, adults would be attending this one, which would, Shannon knew, keep the hijinks to a minimum.

Lauren, beautiful in the slim column of blue, came over to greet Shannon and David. "Okay," she said with a stern expression on her face, "where's the fishnet on the walls? Where are the fake little colored fish hanging from the ceiling? What's going on here?"

David laughed. "Lauren, you are not in a high school gym. This is a class act you're looking at. My mother would give up every bank card she owns before she'd hang fishnet on the walls."

"It's gorgeous," Lauren commented. "I've never seen anything like it."

"Where's the food?" Rick said as he joined them. "I don't see any."

"Gee," Lauren said, "you waited all of five seconds before you asked where the food was. I'm proud of you, Rick. You're making real progress. Now, say hello to Shannon and David."

"Hi. Where's the food?"

"Food's in the Surf Room," David told him. "That gives us more room in here."

Lauren groaned. "The refreshments are in another room?" She glared at Rick. "Will I even get to dance one dance?"

"C'mon," he urged, "let's go check out the feed. Then we'll dance."

"No!" Lauren grabbed his hand. "We're not going anywhere near food until we have at least one dance. I know you, Rick Leon! If you find a table with food on it, you'll stick so close to it people will think you're a waiter! Now get out on that floor and dance or I'll tell everyone here that I beat you at one-on-one. Twice!"

Rick followed her onto the dance floor without another word.

Shannon laughed. "Poor Lauren. I think she'd rather be with Neal."

"Why isn't she?"

Shannon shrugged. She had guessed the reason and she didn't understand it completely, but it wasn't hers to share. "Maybe Rick asked her first."

David looked down at her, taking both her hands in his. "Was there anyone you wish had asked you first?"

"No," she said simply, "there wasn't." But, remembering the second corsage, she wondered uneasily if there was someone out there who thought she should feel differently.

David bent his head to kiss her. She picked up her uneasiness and tossed it away.

Blaine, just entering the ballroom, saw the kiss and made a face of disgust. Gross! Did her brother have to make a spectacle of himself in front of everyone? Okay, so the girl he was with was gorgeous. Not a bad dress, either. Ordinary, of course, but then, Shannon Murphy was ordinary.

Blaine's eyes went straight to Duke, on the bandstand at the front of the room. How he must hate that black tuxedo! She noticed he'd kept his ponytail, though. Good for him. He was intent on his music and hadn't noticed her yet. But she'd definitely see him later.

Glancing again at her brother and Shannon, moving now onto the dance floor, she wondered what had happened to that weird boy with the pale eyes,

the one who had told her Shannon was his girl? She'd
had high hopes for him. She'd been sure that Shannon would never set one foot inside this ballroom.
He must have blown it. She shouldn't be surprised.
He hadn't looked like he had his act together. And
she'd been too frazzled with her own problems to
do anything about Shannon. Too late now.

"Jeff, dance with me," she commanded. She was
annoyed with him. He had flatly refused to wear a
pink tuxedo. "Are you nuts?" he'd cried, as if she
had asked him to shave his head. "I'm not wearing
pink!" And so far tonight, she'd already spotted four
pink tuxedos. Other boys were apparently more co-
operative than Jeff, who was in white.

Something other than his tuxedo color nagged at
her as they walked to the dance floor. Jeff's attitude.
Although she found it hard to believe, he didn't
seem all that thrilled to be with her. "Nice dress"
had been his only comment when she came down
the stairs. He'd said nothing about her hair or her
clever shoes or the antique cameo around her neck,
threaded on black velvet. And what was that look
in his eyes? It wasn't adoration, that was certain.
More like . . . suspicion? Maybe he hadn't bought
her story about Duke being a friend of her father's.
Well, if she'd had more time, she could have come
up with something better. She'd like to get her
hands on the big mouth who had blabbed.

And why was Jeff looking around the room like
that? Searching for something? Jeff wasn't looking
around for some other girl, was he? That was impossible. He belonged to her.

But she could have been one of the ballroom's cream-colored pillars for all the attention Jeff was paying her. He was treating her as if their parents had arranged this date and he had to tolerate her presence or lose his allowance for the next six months. It was positively insulting.

Never mind. She had a traveling musician waiting in the wings.

Jamie and Alex entered the ballroom hand in hand. People passing by them smiled, then sent puzzled glances her way. She grinned. They were having trouble identifying her. Everyone in town knew Jamie Smith, the tennis player. But they were having trouble connecting that person with this Jamie Smith. This was going to be fun!

Alex bowed in front of her. "Miss Smith," he said with exaggerated politeness, "may I have the pleasure of this dance?"

She curtsied, fanning out the folds of her peach-flowered skirt. "You certainly may, sir." She grinned at him. "And the sooner, the better."

Lauren knew Alex Krueger, because he swam at the pool every day. In fact, if she wasn't mistaken, it was *his* head she had narrowly missed the day Neal's younger brothers had sabotaged her on the diving board. But she didn't recognize the girl with him. Pretty dress, very feminine. The peach color was great on her, too. She looked familiar. And *very* happy. Small wonder. Alex wasn't just cute, he was nice, too. Like Neal.

And where, exactly, was Neal? He hadn't changed his mind about attending the ball, had he? Maybe he'd decided that going stag would be a drag. If Neal didn't show up, she'd feel like something important was missing.

"Think they'll have pizza at the food table?" Rick asked as he maneuvered her around a corner.

She stepped on his foot. Hard.

Thad parked the car in his favorite spot, up on the hill overlooking the clubhouse. Shannon would have trouble negotiating the hill if she was wearing high heels. She'd just have to take them off. She could put them back on in the car.

He had looked up the address of the justice of the peace in a neighboring town. Smiling as he carefully made his way down the hill, he wondered if the justice of the peace would ask for a marriage license. Were you supposed to bring that with you when you were getting married? He didn't think so. Didn't people run away and get married on the spur of the moment all the time? The J.P. himself probably had the licenses.

Not concentrating, Thad stumbled in the dark, lost his balance, and fell. He tumbled and rolled down the hill until he slammed into a fallen tree. He cursed as he sat up. He wasn't hurt, but his tux would be filthy. He couldn't walk into the clubhouse now, not looking like this. Someone would take one look at him and call a security guard.

Tears of frustration sprang to his eyes as he stood

up. It wasn't fair. He'd planned so carefully. Every-thing was all set. *Now* look at him!

He tried brushing the leaves and dirt off his tux. The leaves fell to the ground. The dirt stayed. There was no way he could walk into that clubhouse look-ing like he'd been under a car.

Then he remembered the girl. The one with yel-low-white hair, in the red Mercedes. That Hamilton guy's sister. She'd said she didn't want her brother and Shannon to have fun, either. She'd be at the club tonight. And she'd help him. He knew it.

The tux didn't matter. Shannon could help him clean up enough so that the justice of the peace wouldn't throw him out. She wouldn't want to, at first. But when she realized that he loved her enough to go through all of this to get her back, she'd give in. When she understood that he was going to marry her, that he'd made so many plans for them, she'd be really happy. He could see her throwing her arms around his neck and saying, "Oh, Thad! This is so romantic!"

All he had to do now was find a way to get to that Hamilton girl. He couldn't go in to get her. He'd have to think of a way to get her to come outside.

Being more careful now, Thad continued down the hill.

Chapter 17

Blaine had just about had it with Jeffrey Joseph
Christian. Who did he think he was, ignoring her
like this at the biggest dance of the year? She might
as well be one of those stupid palm trees!

"Jeff?"

Nothing. He was sitting opposite her at the table,
but his eyes were on the dance floor. She followed
his gaze. He was looking at . . . a girl! In a flowered
dress. Who *was* she? Blaine had never seen her
before. Or had she? That couldn't be . . . no . . . or
could it? Was that the girl he played tennis with so
often? That Jamie Smith person, the one with all
the trophies? But that Jamie Smith was as plain as
tap water. This one wasn't. If they were one and
the same, someone had introduced her to makeup
and a curling iron. She was actually not bad. And
the boy she was dancing with was cute, in a brainy
sort of way.

"Jeff!"

"What?" But he never even turned his head.
Maybe all that tennis had stolen the swivel from his

neck muscles. The neck she was going to wring if he didn't start paying some attention to her.

Enough! "I'm going to the women's room," she snapped. "If you could manage to stir your bones, maybe you could get me a fresh soda while I'm gone."

"Mmm."

Oh, brother. Blaine jumped up and left the table. Jeff Christian could go jump in the ocean for all she cared. Furious, she stomped toward the women's room. Halfway there, she changed direction as the music stopped and didn't start again. The band was taking a break. Perfect timing! She aimed straight for the bandstand.

Lauren had realized who the pretty girl dancing with Alex Krueger was. Unless her eyesight was deserting her, it was Jamie Smith, the tennis champ. Wow, what a change! She'd always seemed so bony and plain, and quiet as a mouse in class. Not tonight, though. Pretty as a picture, talking to Alex and laughing with him as if she knew everything there was to know about flirting with boys.

That girl, Lauren thought, is obviously having the time of her life. Unlike some of us. And if she can make herself that pretty that quickly, maybe she can make me short.

"Lauren, what are you doing sitting at this table by yourself?"

Watching my fingernails grow, she thought sourly. She looked up.

It was Neal.

She had been this happy to see someone just once before in her life: the time when she was four and she'd slipped away from her mother in a huge department store, becoming hopelessly lost. That time, it had been the security guard whose appearance had overjoyed her, knowing he would reunite her with her mother.

Neal's tuxedo was light blue. Like her gown. Maybe that was a sign that they were meant to be with each other tonight?

She had to lock her legs together under the table to keep from jumping up and throwing her arms around him. Because there was no longer any question in her mind about her feelings for Neal. I love Neal Winthrop, she said to herself. And then, because that made her insides feel like she'd just sipped hot chocolate, she said it again.

But Neal was not her date. "Hi, there," she said very casually, smiling up at him. "Rick went to get something to eat." And eat and eat and eat . . .

Ask me to dance, she commanded silently. I promise I'll say yes. I might slide my shoes off under the table because I'm basically a shallow person, but I will say yes.

He didn't ask her to dance. "I chained my brothers to their beds," he said with a grin. "Just in case you were gearing yourself up for a sneak attack."

"Shame on you," she scolded, wondering if he could hear her heart pounding. "That's child abuse."

Neal shook his head. "No, that's self-protection."

She laughed. But annoyance with herself stopped the laughter. She wanted to be with Neal tonight in this beautiful, romantic place. She wanted to sit with him and dance with him and walk out on the deck with him to look up at the stars. They'd talk and laugh and he'd kiss her. . . . And she could have had every moment of that if she hadn't been such a dimwit.

"Sit?" she asked, hoping he'd say sure. If she knew Rick, he wouldn't be back until he was as stuffed as a Thanksgiving turkey.

Neal shook his head again. Brown hair fell across his forehead. She had to clench her fists to keep from reaching up to brush it back into place. "Better not. Told you — I don't stalk other guys' girls, remember?"

The words, "But I'm *not* Rick's girl and I don't *want* to be," flew to her lips. She caught them in mid-flight. Because if she said that much, she might get completely carried away and add, "I want to be *your* girl."

"Well, have a good time," he said, giving her a casual wave.

Don't go, she telegraphed, looking up and straight into his blue eyes.

He looked back at her for just a minute, un-smiling, as if to say, This was your choice, Lauren, not mine. Then he walked away, into the crowd of dancers surrounding her table.

She couldn't keep herself from glancing down at his feet as he walked away. He hadn't worn the boots, after all. She sagged back in her chair. He wasn't going to ask her to dance, or he would have worn the boots.

She sat at the table alone, kicking herself mentally.

As Thad neared the clubhouse, he hesitated. There was that awful sound . . . the ocean's threatening roar . . . so close. He fought the urge to turn and run. This was a terrifying place to be, but he couldn't leave here until Shannon was at his side where she belonged.

He was too hot in the tuxedo. August was a stupid time of the year to hold a formal dance. Rich or not, Dunes people were not very bright.

His head ached. He needed to think. What was the best way to get to that Hamilton girl without going inside?

He spotted the answer up ahead. A kid in red pants, white shirt, and a ridiculous bow tie at his neck. Parking cars, Thad guessed. He would probably know who Blaine Hamilton was.

Sweating profusely, he hurried over to the boy. Lights from inside the clubhouse shone out over the decks. He saw people dancing, heard the music and the laughter. Shannon was in there somewhere, with all of those people having such a good time. Why wasn't he in there with her?

It didn't matter. Because in just a few minutes, he'd have her back again.

"Could you do me a favor?" he asked when he reached the parking valet.

The boy looked at him, skepticism in his glance.

Aware of his appearance, Thad said quickly, "I was in an accident." He pointed toward the hill. "Up there." Forcing a friendly smile, he added, "I was on my way here. That's why this monkey suit. My date's still in the car. She's okay, but I want to get back to her right away."

The valet relaxed a little then. "You okay, man? No bones broken, I guess, if you made it down the hill on foot."

"I'm okay. Thanks for asking. Listen, you know Blaine Hamilton?"

The boy laughed. "You kidding? Everybody knows Blaine. We call her Blaine-in-the-neck around here." Immediately realizing that he might have made a serious error that could cost him his job, he asked nervously, "You a friend of hers?"

"It's okay," Thad said easily. "I call her that, too. Look, it's like this. Blaine let me borrow her car tonight. It's banged up a little. I can't go inside looking like this, but I need to tell her what happened. Could you go in and bring her out here?"

The boy hesitated and then said, "Sure, I'll go." He glanced down at his watch. "I'm off duty in three minutes, anyway. I'll send Blaine out, then I'll take off. She's with Jeff Christian. Should be easy to find. Oh, who do I tell her is waiting? What's your name, man?"

She'd never remember his name. She might not even remember *him*. "Tell her it's the only guy in Oceanview who hates the ocean."

The boy frowned, then shrugged. "Whatever you say, man. I'll send her out. Good luck with her." And he ran up the wooden stairs and disappeared inside the noisy clubhouse.

And he wasn't coming back. That was great. Getting rid of Blaine after she'd done what he wanted shouldn't be hard, and then he and Shannon would be alone on the beach. Shannon might argue with him at first, just because she wasn't expecting him, and if she did, anyone watching might try to stop him. He couldn't have that.

He began pacing back and forth on the hard-packed sand. Trying to ignore the sound of the pounding surf, he willed Blaine Hamilton to remember him. He had come this far, and made such careful plans. It couldn't all disappear now just because some rich girl had a lousy memory. Not when he was this close.

He watched the clubhouse exit anxiously.

Lauren, still alone at her table, had discovered something she found as intriguing as a good mystery novel. She wasn't the only person in the ballroom trying to keep an eye on someone who was not her date.

Jeff Christian, who had the misfortune, from Lauren's point of view, to be Blaine's date, was busy watching Jamie Smith. Blaine was nowhere around.

Jamie Smith, dancing with Alex Krueger, was watching Jeff watching her.

And earlier, it hadn't escaped Lauren's attention that Blaine had apparently developed a mad passion for music. Particularly the guitar. Particularly when that guitar was being played by a sandy-haired guy in a ponytail.

Everyone seemed to be interested in someone other than their own date.

So, Lauren thought, I have a lot of company. Wasn't anyone with his or her true choice?

At that precise moment, Shannon and David danced by. Her head was resting on his shoulder and he seemed to be whispering in her ear. She smiled in utter contentment, like someone who wouldn't dream of asking anything more from life than what she had at that moment.

Lauren grinned. That answered her question.

Then she thought if she didn't go drag Rick away from *his* true choice — food — she'd have to roll him home like a giant snowball. If you can't get them to dance, she thought with resignation, you might as well join 'em.

She had no idea how lovely she looked walking across the room, head high, a thick mass of dark curls on her shoulders, her steps determined.

Neal could have told her. He watched her every step of the way.

The entrance the parking valet used to go into the clubhouse led him into a dim, narrow hallway behind the bandstand. Which saved him, as it turned out, a great deal of time he might have spent searching for Blaine. Because he almost ran right into her. She was leaning against the wall, half hidden from his view by a guy in a black tuxedo. Because the valet hadn't expected to share the little-used hallway with anyone, he looked carefully to see who it was and what they were doing. To his delight, he recognized her. And there was no question they were kissing. The valet grinned. So where was Jeff Christian, poor guy?

Well, that wasn't any of his business. But this would be a great story to tell his friends. Blaine-in-the-neck would provide a few good laughs. And who deserved it more?

"Hey, Blaine, how's it going?"

"Go away!" Blaine said, pushing the tuxedo away and smoothing her hair. "What are you doing back here, anyway?"

What a witch! The valet grinned wickedly. "Well, not what *you're* doing, that's for sure."

Blaine's blue eyes threw off sparks. "We're just talking, you little jerk! I'm . . . consulting with this musician about selections for the rest of the dance."

"Yeah, sure you are. You wouldn't want to go to the bandleader for that. Anyway, there's a guy outside wants to see you."

Blaine caught her breath. Jeff? He knew she was back here? No, wait a minute. The creep had said "outside." Outside the clubhouse? "Who is it?"

The boy shrugged. "Some guy who says to tell you he's the only guy in Oceanview hates the ocean. He's waiting at the bottom of the wooden stairs, back entrance. Says it's important. Gotta go. Have fun!" he added insolently, and left, pulling off the red bow tie as he went.

It took a minute for his description of the person outside to register. Then she remembered. The pale-eyed boy. The one who'd said he was Shannon's boyfriend. Well, what earthly good did it do to have him show up now? David and Shannon were already here, happy as two kids at Christmastime.

The guy was too late.

The valet, on his way out of the clubhouse, passed Jeff Christian.

"Looking for your girl?" he asked cheerfully. "She's back there, in the hallway. Can't miss her." Grinning happily, he waved and disappeared.

Jeff turned and walked in the direction of the pointed finger.

Chapter 18

Thad Wilcox paced back and forth on the beach. What was keeping that Hamilton girl? Maybe she hadn't remembered him. Maybe that stupid car-park never even looked for her. Maybe . . .

Wasn't that awful roar coming closer? Did the tide come in at night? And if it did, how far up the beach did it come?

He looked up at the lights and the laughter and the music. Shannon, where are you?

His only reply was the slap of water against the shore.

When Jeff came upon Blaine and her musician, it was difficult for him to tell where Blaine ended and the guitar-player began.

He wasn't that surprised. It wasn't as if he'd completely bought her story about this guy being a pal of her dad's. But couldn't she at least have waited until after the ball?

They hadn't noticed him. That didn't surprise him, either.

"Having fun, Blaine?" he said coolly, leaning against the wall a few feet from them.

Blaine jumped, smacking the top of her head on the musician's chin.

Even in the dim light, Jeff could see that she had turned a solid and unattractive beet-red. Clashes with her pink dress, he thought coldly.

"Jeff!" she cried, "how dare you spy on me!"

And wasn't that just like Blaine? Catch her red-handed and she immediately jumped on the person doing the catching. As if *he'd* committed a crime while she was as innocent as that pink-and-white dress tried to make her look. It didn't work.

Why waste time here? He could be looking for Jamie. She wouldn't dump Alex for him, he knew that. She wasn't like Blaine. But she might at least dance with him. And when her date with Alex was over, who knew what could happen? Now that he was free, so to speak.

"See you around," he said, and turned to leave. "I guess you won't have any trouble catching a ride home, right?"

"Wait! Jeff, I — "

"You what?" He waited. Was she going to take a stab at apologizing? Or make up a story that would rival anything concocted by the Brothers Grimm? Neither of those things would work. But it might be a kick to listen.

But Blaine fell silent, her eyes on the floor. She knew a hopeless task when she saw one.

Yanking the pink boutonierre out of his lapel, he

tossed it at her with contempt and left.

"Your boyfriend, I take it," Duke said lazily when Jeff had gone.

She nodded. "That stupid valet must have told him we were back here. I'm going to have that creep fired!"

"Well, that'll teach him." Duke grinned at her.

It wasn't funny. Jeff would never forgive her. Suspecting her was one thing. But catching her at it was something else. Now what was she supposed to do?

She had to look out for herself. If she didn't, who would? "Duke," she said, a coy smile on her face, "you don't really have to leave Oceanview next week, do you? Even if the regular guitarist comes back here, there are other bands in town. You could get a job with one of them." She reached up and touched his cheek, smiling into his eyes. "We could go right on having fun."

He pulled away from her, standing up straight. "Whoa, kiddo!"

She waited, knowing what was coming. This was *not* her night.

"Look, it's been a blast," he said. "Best summer I ever had. But come Tuesday, I'm outa here. You knew that going in. No strings, remember?" He began backing away from her, as if she were reaching out with handcuffs. "Take my advice and go make up with your boyfriend. Just turn on the charm. That'll do it."

Was he crazy? Hadn't he seen how angry Jeff had been?

"Look, I've gotta get back to work." He paused, then added, "And this is *it*, right here and now, okay? Don't come back here after the dance. Farewell scenes are not my thing. So long!"

And he was gone.

Blaine stared after him in disgust. Faster than a speeding bullet, she had gone from having two guys interested in her to none. She clenched her teeth. They were both jerks! They had totally ruined the ball for her.

Laughter and music from the ballroom made her feel nauseated. A good time was being had by all. Except her. And her parents practically ran the place. It wasn't fair.

Just exactly what was she supposed to do now?

The pale-eyed boy. Shannon's ex-boyfriend. A clear vision of him suddenly popped into her head. Okay, so what had just happened wasn't David's fault. Or Shannon's. But why should they have a good time when she couldn't? They weren't so special. She couldn't stand the thought of their happiness when she was so miserable. Maybe it was too late to get David out of that girl's clutches. Then again, maybe it wasn't.

It wasn't as if she had anything better to do just now.

A wicked glint appeared in Blaine's blue eyes. She would be doing David a favor by blitzing his relationship with that girl.

She hesitated. Would the guy still be there? It had been a while since that valet had given her his message and then gone tattling to Jeff. Maybe Shannon's ex-boyfriend had given up and run along home.

There was only one way to find out.

Blaine smoothed her hair, straightened her gown, and went in search of the only boy in town who hated the ocean.

Jamie was dancing in Alex's arms when she saw Jeff come out from behind the bandstand. His handsome face was twisted with disgust.

The bandstand? She'd bet every trophy she owned that he'd caught Blaine in a game of musical chairs. Poor Jeff, she thought. He'd probably stumbled onto exactly the same scene that Jamie had found at the tennis court. How awful for him! She was furious with Blaine. How could she hurt Jeff like that?

Who are you kidding? the little voice inside her head sneered. You haven't been this thrilled since last Christmas and you know it. So cut out the act! You're already trying to figure out how to console him. Which makes *you* almost as rotten as Blaine. In case you've forgotten, Alex Krueger brought you to this dance. Remember him? He's the guy who's smiling at you right this very minute.

She looked up guiltily. "Having a good time?" he asked.

"Yes!" she answered too quickly and too loudly. "Everything is wonderful. I've never had so much fun." Well, that was true enough. She hadn't exactly logged a lot of hours of funtime in her life. But even if she had, she knew that tonight would still be special. The ballroom was a shimmering, glimmering fairyland, the music great, and Alex was fun to be with.

"You have the greatest smile," he said, holding her close.

What was the matter with her, anyway? When had Jeff Christian ever complimented her smile, or anything else about her before tonight? Never, that's when. And the fact that he'd been looking her way all evening didn't mean that she should forget about Alex. That would make her almost as rotten as Blaine.

"Thank you," she said, hugging him back.

"When this dance is over, how about if we go eat?" Alex said, his lips brushing against her hair. "Can't live on love," he added lightly, "or so they tell me."

Love? "Fine with me." Better to eat than discuss love, something she was not at all prepared for.

Where had Jeff gone? Home? She couldn't help hoping he hadn't.

He hadn't. He was at the refreshment table, filling a plate. From the look of it, whatever he'd learned about Blaine hadn't destroyed his appetite. And Jamie noticed with satisfaction that he didn't seem all bent out of shape. The tone of his voice as he talked to Lauren was normal. Shannon Murphy and David Hamilton were eating, too. Lauren's date, a boy Jamie recognized as a well-known area basketball player, sat slumped in a chair. He looked like he was about to fall asleep. An empty plate perched precariously on his lap.

"Maybe I should just plop a lampshade on Rick's head," Lauren suggested, glaring at him. "It would hide his identity. No one would know that's *my* date who ate himself into semi-unconsciousness. I, personally, would still be mortified, but at least no one would know why."

David laughed.

Jamie didn't. Poor Lauren. And she looked so beautiful in her blue gown, like a model or a movie star.

"You should have come with Neal," she heard Shannon tell Lauren softly. "He would never act like such a clod."

Lauren sighed ruefully. "Tell me about it. I'm an idiot." She patted her stomach. "And I'm a hungry idiot. Fortunately for all of us, the human vacuum cleaner here," she said, nodding toward Rick, "zonked out before devouring every last crumb. Let's get to it, quick, before he comes to and realizes his mistake."

Laughing, they attacked the table.

Outside, Blaine was staring, open-mouthed, at Thad Wilcox. His appearance shocked and disgusted her. It occurred to her that she might have made her second mistake of the evening by coming out here alone.

"Where have you been?" he cried. "I've been waiting here forever!"

"I just got your message," she lied. "What do you want, anyway? David and Shannon are already inside, having the time of their lives. I thought you were going to take care of things *before* the dance."

He shook his head. "No, this is better. This is perfect. I'm going to take Shannon away from here, and then your brother will understand that he can't take whatever he wants, not when it belongs to someone else."

This guy must have been dropped on his head when he was a baby. "Shannon's not a thing," she reminded him tartly. "She's a person, and if you could see what a great time she's having, you'd understand that coming here with him was her own choice." Not that she, Blaine, was all that happy about Shannon's choice. She wasn't. But this guy's eyes looked wild, as if they didn't belong to a civilized person. It wouldn't hurt to calm him down a little. If possible.

His body went rigid. "I don't want to hear that! She didn't know what she was doing. Your brother confused her."

Shannon hadn't looked confused to her. "How would you get Shannon away from the ball, anyway?" she heard herself ask. She blamed it on simple curiosity. "She won't come with you. Not the way you look right now."

"She's not coming outside with me. She's coming outside with *you*."

"Me?" She shook her head. He was talking about practically kidnaping Shannon. And he expected her to help? "Forget it!"

His eyes became slivers of ice. He grabbed her wrist. "You promised!" he reminded her in a nasty whisper. "You said you'd help."

She must have looked frightened, because he quickly dropped her wrist and apologized. "Look," he said softly, "I'm sorry. But this is important. I've made plans. Shannon belongs with *me*, not your brother."

Well, that was certainly true enough. And from the way David and Shannon had looked tonight, somebody had better do something fast or they'd be welded together permanently. I cannot, she thought emphatically, have a Murphy for an in-law.

A chorus of laughter from the clubhouse set her teeth on edge. They were all having so much fun, including David and Shannon. It wasn't fair!

"What do you want me to do?"

"Just get her out of there. Tell her you're sick and you need air or something. She's a nice person. She'll help you out. I'll do the rest."

"You're not going to hurt her, are you?" David would never forgive her if anything happened to Shannon.

Thad looked as if she'd slapped him. "You just don't get it, do you? I *love* Shannon. And she loves me. It's your brother who's messing everything up for us. Now go and get her. Hurry up!"

Maybe Shannon really did love him. Of course David had more money. To a girl like that, money could make all the difference. Or maybe she was just confused, like Thad said. Whatever. Blaine wasn't going to keep arguing with a guy who looked like a couple of his burners had gone out. "Okay, okay! Relax! I'll see what I can do."

She turned and ran up the stairs.

Finding Shannon was no problem. David's blond head towered over most of the other dancers.

She might have changed her mind then if they hadn't looked so disgustingly romantic. Remembering the angry look on Jeff's face when he caught her with Duke, she told herself that David had no right to be so happy when his own sister was miserable. Where was his family loyalty, anyway?

She tapped on his arm. "David. David!" For Pete's sake, were these two on another planet? What did she have to do to get his attention, set off fireworks in the middle of the dance floor? Thad was right — they were breaking up this cozy twosome just in time. "DAVID!"

"What?" Annoyance lay heavy on that single word. "What do you want?"

"I'm sick, David. I need some air and I can't find Jeff." A bald-faced lie. There he was, big as life, dancing with that girl in the old-fashioned dress. But David's back was to him and he wasn't aware that Jeff was so close. "Can Shannon come outside with me for a few minutes? Please?"

Shannon was stunned by the request. Blaine hadn't even acknowledged her existence before this moment. If she needed help, shouldn't she go to a friend?

And then Shannon decided it wasn't at all likely that Blaine *had* any friends. Not any that were close enough to be willing to leave this dance for her. That was probably the price of being an incorrigible flirt.

"I'll go with you," David offered.

"No!" Blaine burst out. "I . . . I might get sick and I don't want any guy around when I do."

"I'm your brother."

"You're still a guy."

"I'll go with her," Shannon said. She and Blaine would never be friends, but she *was* David's sister and maybe helping her out would wipe that perpetual sneer off her upper lip, the one she wore whenever she looked at Shannon. "You go get something to drink," she told David. "We'll be right back."

"Thanks, Shannon," Blaine gushed, grabbing Shannon's hand. "Outside, quick!"

Shannon followed Blaine outside.

If someone had asked, David wouldn't have been able to explain the feeling of uneasiness that crept over him then. His date had just gone outside with his sister. Nothing sinister in that. He was being silly.

To block out the feeling, he took Shannon's advice. He left the ballroom for the Surf Room and its refreshment table.

Chapter 19

Lauren had had better times in a dentist's chair than she was having at the Drifting Dunes Sandcastles Ball. Having a cavity filled seemed infinitely less painful than being at a great dance like this one with the wrong person, especially when the *right* person was sitting directly across the room trying to pretend she didn't exist.

The "right person" got up and asked a cute blonde to dance.

"I'm getting kind of hungry again," Rick said. They had danced exactly three dances all night long. So much for dancing romantically with someone she could look up to. Every time she'd looked up at Rick, he'd been chewing something. He couldn't possibly be hungry. Maybe he had a metabolic imbalance or something. Or maybe he was just bored. She could certainly understand that.

"Well, of course you are." Lauren yanked her eyes away from Neal. "You haven't eaten a thing in the last seven minutes. There must be an inch or two in your left ankle that isn't filled up yet."

Sarcasm went right over Rick's head. He stood up, all six feet, three inches of him. She was not impressed. So he was tall. Big deal. Trees were tall, but you wouldn't take one to a ball, would you?

"I'm not hungry. I'm not eating again until Thanksgiving. But you go ahead. I wouldn't want my date passing out from malnutrition."

"Okay. Be right back."

Lauren settled back in her chair, pasting a phony smile on her face. Neal would be dancing by her table any second now. She had to look as if she was having the time of her life. It was bad enough that he knew perfectly well why she was attending this dance with the Great American Garbage Disposal — having him feel sorry for her would make her want to crawl under the floor-length tablecloth and hide there the rest of the night.

She smiled brilliantly as Neal, the blonde in his arms, danced by her table. She decided happily that the girl looked a little bit like a French poodle. All that tightly curled hair all over her head, like loops of yarn.

Oh, Lauren, she scolded, you are a truly evil person! But a wicked giggle accompanied the scolding.

On the beach, Shannon stared in disbelief as Thad came out of his hiding place under the wooden stairs and confronted her, a triumphant smile on his pale, unshaven face. Her bewildered eyes took in his disheveled appearance. What was he doing here?

"I've come for you, Shannon," he said softly,

moving toward her. The breeze off the water failed to budge a single strand of his unwashed hair. "You knew I would, didn't you?" Then, politely, "Thanks, Blaine. You can go now."

Blaine? Shannon whirled to face her. The skirt of her gown whirled with her. "You *knew* he was out here!" she accused. "Blaine, this is crazy! You don't know — "

"This is between the two of you," Blaine interrupted, backing away from Shannon. To Thad, she said, "I did my part. The rest is up to you." And she turned and ran up the wooden stairs, holding up the hem of her pink-and-white dress as she ran.

"Blaine!" Shannon called, frantic at the thought of being left alone with Thad. "Tell David where I am! Blaine!"

But the click-clack of Blaine's custom-made shoes on the wooden stairs faded quickly and then disappeared entirely.

Shannon was alone on a quiet, deserted beach with a boy who had sent her dead flowers.

Jamie, wrapped in Jeff Christian's arms on the dance floor, decided that the reason she wasn't thrilled to pieces to be dancing with him again was that he had started talking tennis. He hadn't, at first. During their first dance together he'd spent the entire time telling her how pretty she looked, which would have pleased her more if he hadn't sounded so surprised.

Then he'd told her, repeatedly, what a fool he'd been. This was true, of course, so she hadn't argued with him. But everyone knew that Jeff had stumbled on Blaine and that guitar player and they hadn't been discussing music. So the question was, if Jeff hadn't discovered how treacherous Blaine was, would she, Jamie, still be in these arms?

She wasn't at all sure of the answer.

The amazing thing was, Jeff was trying to make all of this tennis talk romantic!

He murmured into her ear, "If you help me with my backhand, it'll give us a good excuse to spend more time together."

Jamie lifted her head. Wasn't he assuming an awful lot? Did he really think she'd been waiting with bated breath for him to dump Blaine? Had he forgotten that she'd come to this ball with someone else?

"Tomorrow afternoon?" he asked, looking into her eyes. "You busy?"

He's absolutely positive that I'm not, she thought with certainty. She saw Alex standing just off the dance floor with a girl in a red dress. A very pretty girl in a red dress. "I don't know yet," she said deliberately. "Why don't you call me in the morning?"

"Oh."

Oh, what? Oh, I can't believe you have other plans? Or, Oh, you foolish girl, playing hard-to-get?

The music ended. "Thanks for the dance," Jeff said, the tiniest of frowns creasing his forehead. She had surprised him with her response. Well, good. Being taken for granted was something she intended to put behind her. Very far behind her.

"Thad, let *go* of me!" Shannon ordered, her voice shaky. His grip on her wrist might as well have been steel handcuffs.

"No. Can't do that. We have to hurry. My car is up there." He pointed to the hill beyond the clubhouse. In the darkness, it seemed foreign and menacing to Shannon, although she knew that hill well.

"I'm not going *anywhere* with you." Shannon's eyes frantically searched the beach. Nothing. No one. Why wasn't anyone out walking on such a lovely night?

Because everyone was at the dance and not about to tackle a sandy beach in high heels.

"You are coming with me," Thad corrected. "And you won't be sorry. I have a surprise for you." He tugged on her wrist.

She dug her heels into the sand. Safety was here, at the foot of the clubhouse stairs. Someone could come outside at any moment, see her struggling with Thad, and run to her rescue. Away from here, though, she would be totally on her own with someone who actually believed she would enjoy a surprise from him.

But their tug-of-war over her wrist was tearing at her skin. Tiny droplets of blood appeared on the surface. "Thad, look what you're doing!" she cried, hoping to shock him into releasing her.

"It's your own fault," he said calmly. "Stop fighting me. I know what's best for you, Shannon. That's because I love you." He said the words grimly.

He gave one powerful yank on her tortured wrist

and her heels came up out of the sand. The laughter and the music were tantalizingly close but of no use to her. Shannon felt herself being dragged away from the safety of the clubhouse.

And there was nothing she could do to stop it.

Trying to avoid both her brother and her ex-date was proving a challenge even for someone as clever as Blaine. David was at one end of the ballroom, talking to a friend, and Jeff was near the bandstand at the opposite end. She decided to avoid the ballroom completely until Thad had time to get Shannon away from there. While she was inventing a super story to lay on David about Shannon's disappearance, she might as well eat. She turned and went into the Surf Room.

The only person at the refreshment table who looked interesting was a tall, dark-haired guy whose plate looked like Mount Everest. No adoring female at his side. Good. She was in desperate need of an escort. Hard to believe, but true. She had no intention of sitting out the rest of this ball. The very second she thought it was safe to do so, she was zipping back to the ballroom and dancing the night away. For that, she needed a partner.

Was he really going to *eat* all of that? His cummerbund must be elastic. "Hi!" she said, picking up a gold-rimmed white china plate and smiling up at him brilliantly. "I'll just bet you play basketball."

In the ballroom, a roll of drums heralded the announcement of this year's Sandcastles Queen. All laughter and chattering stopped. Several girls with high hopes of receiving the honor dragged their dates closer to the bandstand, as if being in the immediate vicinity of the announcer might make all the difference.

Harper Hamilton approached the microphone. His wavy, silver hair contrasted beautifully with his black tuxedo. "Good evening, ladies and gentlemen," he began jovially. "I hope you're all having a wonderful time. I know *I* am."

Lauren, still sitting alone, wasn't listening. She was searching the room for Neal. She finally found him, sitting alone at a table.

"It is my pleasure," Blaine's father said, "to announce the name of this year's Sandcastles Queen. The judges assure me it was a very difficult choice. But their selection was unanimous." He turned to the bandleader. "Maestro, another drum roll, please."

The bandleader obliged.

Lauren, catching Neal's eye, smiled.

He smiled back.

Harper Hamilton turned back to the microphone. "Our Sandcastles Queen is . . . Miss Lauren Marie Tolliver!"

There was applause. Lauren didn't hear it. She was busy wondering if she stared straight at Neal willing him to come to her, would he do it?

Harper looked around the room. The guests, young and old, did the same. No Sandcastles Queen had squealed with delight. No one was approaching the stage. He repeated his announcement. "Our

Queen is Miss Lauren Marie Tolliver. Miss Tolliver? Are you with us?"

Neal started laughing. Lauren frowned. Was he laughing at her? For staring at him? Scarlet with embarrassment, she tore her eyes from his and returned to the real world. Why was everyone standing around like that? And were they staring at her? They certainly seemed to be.

"Lauren!" Silly stood over her. "Are you deaf? You've been picked to be Queen. Get yourself up on the stage. He's called your name twice."

Queen? Called her name? Twice? No wonder Neal had been laughing. What a goose she was! Queen? Well!

Lauren stood up, slapped an appropriately regal smile on her face and, head high, walked to the bandstand amid thunderous applause.

Chapter 20

Shannon moved slowly, as if she were plodding through molasses. Impatient with her, Thad dragged her by her wrist so vigorously that she cried out in pain.

"Sorry," he said sullenly, "but you're going too slow. We have to get up the hill before your boyfriend comes looking for you. Now, hurry up!"

David. He *would* come looking for her, wouldn't he? But how could she slow Thad down? He was frantic with the need to hurry.

She had only one chance. To get to the water. To those breakers roaring in the distance. If she could make it to the surf, Thad would never follow her into the water. And she could hide in there, among the waves she knew so well, a long time if she had to. Until someone came to help.

But his grip on her wrist was iron-clad. And he would never let her go voluntarily.

Okay, Shannon thought with a sudden fierce rage, so let it be *in*voluntarily. Who did he think she was, dragging her along the beach like a sack of potatoes? As if she were a thing, not a person. And babbling the whole time about how happy they'd be when they were married. Married! She didn't even *like* the guy.

A plan. She needed a plan.

"I have to take off my sandals," she whined. "I can't walk on the sand in these silly things." So why are they called *sandals*, she felt like adding, but didn't. Thad had no sense of humor.

He was willing to do anything to speed things up. "Go ahead," he said, keeping a close watch on her every move.

She bent down and with her free hand, unfastened her left shoe. Leaving it on the sand, she reached over to her right foot. Gripping that shoe tightly in her left hand, she deftly turned it so the heel pointed upright. Then, in one swift motion, she brought both her body and the shoe up straight. There was no time to aim. She thrust the pointed heel at Thad's face with all her might, connecting with the underside of his nose, the soft part just above his upper lip. Blood spurted. He screamed. And let go of her wrist.

Shannon took off in her stocking feet, yanking the folds of her dress up around her knees, and raced across the beach toward the water, red hair flying out behind her as she ran.

Lauren stood on the bandstand, clutching the beautiful spray of deep red roses and white baby's breath Harper Hamilton had handed her. Applause and a few whistles came from the crowd around the stage. She found herself wishing her parents were part of that crowd, witnessing this triumphant moment. Because her mother had been right. More than once, when Lauren was sulking about her height, her mother had said calmly, "Your turn will come. How many short beauty queens have you seen?" Lauren giggled softly to herself, standing on the stage in the spotlight. Am I a beauty queen? she wondered. Me? Well, she was carrying a bouquet of roses and wearing a silver crown on her head, so she guessed she was. At least for tonight.

And where was her date while she was reigning in glory? Was he standing at her feet, gazing up at her with adoration and pride? He was *not*. Off sampling the zucchini muffins, no doubt.

Then she spied him. He had just entered the ballroom, probably, she thought, to see what all the commotion was about. He carried a plate in his hand and Blaine Hamilton was at his elbow, as close as she could be.

So. Blaine was up to her old tricks: off with the old, on with the new. Rumor had it that she and Jeff had had some sort of falling-out. Leave it to Blaine to latch on to someone tall, dark, and handsome . . . and hungry. Lauren giggled again. At least Blaine had the money to keep Rick in groceries.

"You and your escort will start off this dance," Harper Hamilton said. "The rest of us will join you after you've circled the room once."

Lauren smiled. The music began. It was a slow, mellow piece, the kind of music you want to dance to with someone you care a lot about. A slow dance.

Lauren did not step out of her high heels. She ignored the fact that the silver crown perched on her dark waves added another two inches to her height. She left the stage and walked straight across the room to where Neal sat alone at a table. He looked up and frowned as she approached, her heart pounding. She was taking a big chance here. What if he said no? She wouldn't blame him. But it would be horribly embarrassing, with everyone watching.

I could order him to dance with me, she thought giddily. I'm a queen, after all.

"Neal," she said softly over the music, "may I have this dance?"

He was surprised, she could see it in his eyes. He had thought she was headed straight for Rick. And for one tiny, horrible second, she thought he was going to tell her to do just that. "You have a date," he would say. "Why are you bothering *me?*"

And she would march straight outside and throw herself off the deck.

He didn't say that. He stood up. No one giggled at the difference in their height. "Are you sure?" was all that he said.

She nodded, her eyes on his. "I'm sure."

Then, "I'd like that very much," he said with dignity and a warm smile.

There was a second round of applause then, as they moved onto the dance floor and Lauren walked into Neal's arms.

Rick said to Blaine, his mouth full, "She's supposed to be my date! How come she's dancing with Winthrop?"

Blaine patted his arm. "Don't worry about it. Blaine will take good care of you. Why don't we just go see if there's any cake left?"

She wanted to get out of the ballroom before David spotted her.

Too late. Here he came, and he looked like a man with a mission. She hadn't invented an excuse yet for Shannon's absence. She'd just have to wing it. What difference did it make now? Shannon was gone. David was safe.

"Where's Shannon?" David demanded. "She hasn't come back yet. And why aren't you with her? I thought you were sick."

She excused herself to Rick, who barely noticed, and pulled her brother into a quiet corner. "I hate to tell you this, but Shannon left."

"Left?"

"Um-hmm. With her old boyfriend." Blaine shook her head regretfully. She thought that was a nice touch. "I guess they'd had a fight before you met her. But he came to get her tonight, and they made up. And . . ." she spread her hands helplessly ". . . well, what can I say? Can't argue with true love, can we?"

Her brother's blue eyes narrowed suspiciously. "*What* old boyfriend?"

"Someone named . . . um, Thad Wilcox, I think. I guess they went together for a long time. She was probably just using you to make him jealous." She pursed her lips in disapproval. "Some girls do that, David."

"Not Shannon."

Blaine lost her patience. "Oh, how can you be so sure? You hardly know that girl!"

"I know she wouldn't just take off like that without saying anything." David was remembering Shannon's strange behavior when they'd first met — how jumpy she'd seemed, how she wouldn't let him take her home, how reluctant she'd been to let their relationship develop. As if . . . as if she'd been afraid of something. Or someone?

Why hadn't he seen it? What was the matter with him? Big genius, can't even figure out that a girl is scared to death!

And Blaine hadn't been ill at all. The whole thing had been a set-up, and his sister was in it up to her neck. "You're lying!" he accused. "Admit it! You weren't sick. Something's going on that you know about. Tell me what it is before I wring your conniving little neck!"

"Blaine," Rick called from a few feet away, "I don't feel so hot. I think I need to sit down."

"Sure, Rick," eager to escape David's enraged gaze, "be right there."

"NO!"

David's outburst startled her. She hadn't known he had it in him. He was supposed to be the "easygoing" one in the family.

He grabbed her arm. "You're not moving one step until you tell me exactly what's going on."

Oh, well, why not? Thad and that girl were probably long gone by now, anyway. "It wasn't my fault. He tricked me. He said he just wanted to tell her to have a good time. And I believed him. I felt sorry for him. After all," she added snidely, "that girl dumped him for you, just because you have more money. Anyone would feel sorry for him."

"Yeah," David said sarcastically, "that compassion of yours gets you in trouble all the time, doesn't it?"

Blaine didn't even blush.

"Where are they?" her brother demanded. "Where did you take Shannon?"

"They're probably not there now, David. Why don't you just forget about her?"

"WHERE?"

"Oh, all right! If you're determined to make a fool of yourself over that girl. They were on the beach. Near the back stairs. But I'm sure they're gone by now. You're just wasting your time."

He was gone so fast his tuxedo blurred in front of her eyes. Blaine felt a stab of jealousy. What did the Murphy girl have, to inspire such deep feelings in not one, but *two* guys?

"Blaine!" Rick was beginning to look a little green around the edges.

"I'm coming." What was she, a nurse? Just because he'd made a disgusting pig of himself, she was probably going to miss that last dance.

This event was not turning out at all the way she'd planned. It was all that stupid car-park's fault. First thing in the morning, that idiot was out of a job!

But that wouldn't do a thing to fix tonight, would it?

A phony look of concern plastered across her face, she went back to Rick.

Lauren, dancing with Neal, saw David rush out of the ballroom. What was going on? She hadn't seen Shannon in a while, either. Whatever was happening, she'd bet her crown Blaine was behind it.

Well, she wasn't going to let Blaine-in-the-neck spoil this wonderful, magical night. Because she had discovered to her delight that she could dance with someone shorter than herself very comfortably. Very contentedly. Very romantically.

She forgot about Blaine and David and Shannon and Rick and closed her eyes.

Shannon, her breath coming in painful gasps, reached the surf. She no longer heard Thad's footsteps pounding behind her. But she didn't dare turn her head to make sure he was no longer pursuing her. She had to keep going. And only after she was deep in the safety of the ocean that Thad hated would she turn and look.

Taking a deep breath, she dove into the pounding waves.

Chapter 21

Jamie, still with Jeff after their last dance together, watched as Lauren marched over to Neal and asked him to dance. And then Jamie held her breath as Neal stood up. Would everyone laugh? Lauren was wearing heels. Neal wasn't.

No one laughed. Jamie relaxed. And the funny thing was, Lauren and Neal looked good together out there on the dance floor. Both in blue, holding each other closely, they seemed to be in a world of their own, where measuring tapes didn't count.

Jamie glanced around her. All of the adults were smiling at the couple gliding across the dance floor. She grinned. That's the older generation for you, she thought. They know real romance when they see it.

She decided the judges' choice had been a good one. She had thought they would pick Shannon Murphy, who looked so radiant tonight. But Lauren did have a regal air about her. And it must have taken the courage of a real queen to ask Neal to dance. Lauren deserved that crown.

Lauren was having more fun than she, Jamie, was. All Jeff had talked about for the last fifteen minutes was tennis.

Where was Alex?

Alex was coming, just then, from the Surf Room, where he'd tried to eat. Everyone had said the refreshments were delicious. To him, they tasted like seaweed.

Because it was so obvious that Jamie had a thing for Jeff Christian. Anyone could see it. He didn't blame her. The two of them had a lot in common. It probably wasn't much fun for Jamie, being with someone who couldn't tell a lob from a volley. Alex's lips tightened. Even for her, this funny, pretty girl in the flowered dress, he was *not* ready to take up tennis. She might as well know that right now. Then she could make an "informed choice," as his debate coach would put it. His face grim, he started across the room toward her.

". . . And it seems to me there's something about the way you grip the handle," Jeff was telling Jamie in an earnest voice. "Maybe you could show me exactly how you do that. Which fingers apply the most pressure, that kind of thing."

Jamie saw Alex approaching, saw the look on his face, and thought fast. She had loved Jeff for a long time. Now it looked like she could have him if she wanted him. But Alex had liked her before her make-over. Alex had liked her when she was still "plain as a mud fence," to quote her grandmother. And Alex didn't care two hoots for her backhand or her forehand or her trophies. He only cared about her. What sort of crazy person would ask for more than that?

And when she finally laid down her racket for good, Jeff might disappear. He might take his tennis balls and go home.

But Alex wouldn't.

". . . I wanted to ask you," Jeff continued, "if you are really happy with the club's referees. Seems to me a couple of them don't know what they're doing."

Alex stood before Jamie. "I want you to know," he said stiffly, "that I will probably never pick up a tennis racket as long as I live."

Jamie flashed him the brilliant smile that had led to their first date. "Well, I should hope not!" she said emphatically. "One tennis freak in this twosome is enough. Besides," she added softly, taking his hand, "all that running around out there in the hot sun could ruin your dancing. I would hate that." She looked into his eyes and saw both relief and happiness there. "Dancing," she said, "is such a good excuse for you to put your arms around me."

"I don't need an excuse," he said, taking both of her hands and drawing her onto the dance floor. "Do I?"

"No," she said. "You don't."

Alex knew that she had made her choice.

"Jamie?" Jeff called after them, his voice bewildered. "Jamie?"

But Alex and Jamie went right on dancing.

Blaine, sitting with Rick, who moaned every three or four minutes, wondered exactly when this evening had gone sour on her. The dress and shoes were perfect, her hair had never looked better, her makeup was holding up beautifully. But all of these people were having a great time dancing, laughing, talking . . . and here she sat, with a guy she hardly knew and wouldn't ordinarily have bothered with, a guy who thought of nothing but his stupid stomach!

How had that happened?

Blaine sighed. "Wait here," she ordered. "I'll go get you something from the kitchen for your stomach." She wasn't doing it for him. She was doing it for herself. Because she was going to dance that last dance even if she had to prop this guy up with two-by-fours!

Shannon had discovered very quickly that swimming in a long gown was nearly impossible. The thick folds of the skirt had wrapped themselves around her ankles, imprisoning her legs. Floating in the salty waves, she reached down with one hand and yanked with all her might, pulling the sodden fabric free. It would wrap itself around her again, but there was no way she could slip out of the gown now. She'd just have to keep yanking it up.

Temporarily free of the skirt, she used long, sure strokes to cut her way through the water and get far beyond the beach. When she felt completely safe, she turned to look for Thad. Just one glimpse of him running up the hill alone would be enough to set her mind at ease.

Out where she was, it was pitch-black. If there

was a moon, it was hidden behind clouds. But there were lights scattered about the beach, and with any luck at all one of them would cast its glow over Thad.

She saw nothing. Facing the beach as she floated, she peered into the darkness, her eyes darting back and forth along the beach, searching frantically. Where was he?

She saw no movement on the beach.

Could he have made it off the beach and up the hill so quickly? Wouldn't he have waited on the beach to see if she might come right back? He'd seemed so determined to take her with him.

Then she heard it. A sound so faint, at first she thought it was just a summer breeze blowing across the water.

It came again. A wail, very like the wind, but undeniably human.

And then, directing her eyes toward the sound, she saw him. Thad. In the water. Floundering, in the ocean that he hated so passionately. His hands were beating at the surface as if to push the water away.

It couldn't be. He would never, never jump into the ocean. She knew he wouldn't. She had been counting on that to save her.

But there he was. And he was in trouble.

The wail became a word, clearly heard now. "Help! Help!"

He would drown. She knew that as surely as she knew that only she could save him. He couldn't swim, had never learned. And even capable swimmers often floundered in the sea, overwhelmed by its awesome power. Thad had always been over-whelmed by it. He wouldn't even try to swim, al-though she'd coaxed him more than once.

So he would drown.

Had he been so desperate that even the thought of almost-certain death by drowning hadn't kept him from following her? But that wasn't love. That was obsession. And they weren't the same thing at all.

For just one infinitesimal moment — a moment Shannon would never share with anyone for as long as she lived — she thought about not saving him. Anyone who had done what Thad had just done was suicidal. Maybe letting him go would be doing him a favor . . . and she would never have to worry about him or be frightened of him again.

The moment passed as quickly as it had come, as if it had never even taken shape in her mind. Shaking salt water from her eyes, Shannon yanked at her skirt again, and with its folds clear of her legs, began swimming in earnest. Toward Thad.

Thad had hesitated at the water's edge for long, agonizing minutes after Shannon escaped from him and dove into the waves. His nose was bleeding and painful, his heart was pounding wildly, his legs were weak. He couldn't do it. Not even for Shannon. He couldn't jump into the powerful waves with their deep, dark secrets. Something terrible would hap-pen to him in there. Something slithery and sinister might be waiting for him, as it always was in dark places.

And then he realized that it didn't matter. Because Shannon didn't want him anymore. She really didn't. She wouldn't have argued with him or bloodied his nose or run into the ocean if she cared anything about him at all. She had ruined her beautiful dress and her pretty hairdo, just to avoid him.

Life without Shannon would be empty and cold and dark.

So what did it matter what might be out there?

He began walking into the shallows. She would try to save him, he knew that. That was the kind of person she was. But he'd fight her. He'd fight hard. Salt water licked at his feet, at the dress shoes he had borrowed from the floor of his father's closet. Very quickly, so quickly it took his breath away, the water swallowed his knees, his thighs. But no chilling terror filled him, no horror of the sea. He felt . . . nothing. Without Shannon to love him, nothing mattered.

He kept on walking.

When David reached the foot of the wooden stairs, his eyes swept the beach. It was as deserted as it would be in mid-January. He turned to scan the hill. Nothing. Was he too late? Could that guy have taken Shannon away? Where would he have taken her? And how would he, David, ever find her? Why hadn't she *told* him about this guy? Why was she afraid to tell him? And why hadn't he guessed?

He called her name, not expecting an answer. Then called it again, louder this time. No answer.

Just the sound of the waves and the music and laughter from above him.

He began walking up the beach, trying to decide what to do. Call the police? Go to the guy's house? What was his name . . . Wilcox? Blaine could give him the name, and *would*, if she wanted to live to celebrate her next birthday.

He stumbled upon something lying on the sand. Reaching down, he picked up the object. A shoe. A black sandal with a high heel. And here was its mate, a few feet away, lying on its side.

Shannon had been wearing black shoes. He remembered because she'd tripped going up the wooden stairs and he'd been afraid she'd sprained her ankle. She had laughed and wiggled her toes to show him she was fine. These were the shoes, he was sure of it. And one of them had blood on it.

Holding the shoes in his hands, David began to run.

"I hope you won't mind, Rick," Lauren told the tall, greenish-faced boy by Blaine's side, sitting with his hands over his stomach, "but I'm going home with Neal." Queens, she figured, had some special rights. Certainly the right to pick one's escort was high on that list. It had taken some doing to convince Neal that he wasn't "stealing" her, that Rick had other things on his mind besides her, and wouldn't even miss her. She wasn't giving up now.

Rick moaned, his hands clutching his cummer-bunded middle. "Blaine, you got any more of that club soda?" To Lauren, he said, "Yeah, sure. Go ahead. Blaine'll take me home." He groaned again. "If I survive."

"Oh, you'll live," Blaine said tartly. "And you'll probably want to stop for something to eat on the way home."

Lauren laughed. It sounded like Blaine had Rick's number. "Blaine, have you seen Shannon? And David? I can't find them anywhere. Didn't I see Shannon leave with you a while ago?"

Blaine suddenly became very interested in the small ceramic sandcastle on the table. "Have you ever seen such cute candleholders? I wonder how they made these?"

"Blaine!" Lauren fixed a steely gaze on Blaine's pretty face. "Is something going on with them? Tell me!" she commanded.

Blaine shrugged. Lauren didn't make as great a queen as *she* had. Her hair was too . . . loose. What queen ever let her hair flop around like that? It should be upswept. The girl had no class. "They might be down on the beach. Maybe." She stood up. "I'll go get you some more soda, Rick." Anything to get away from Lauren's suspicious gaze.

"C'mon, Neal," Lauren said as Blaine flounced away, "let's go see what's keeping David and Shannon away from my dance."

"Yes, your majesty," he said with a grin and a bow. "But if we don't find them, can we stay on the beach for a while? I wouldn't mind a private audience with royalty."

Lauren laughed. "I just might grant that wish. As long as we're back here for the last dance. I don't want to miss it."

Another bow. "Your every wish is my command."

Laughing, they aimed for the exit to the beach.

Shannon wasted no time in reaching a now thoroughly terrified Thad, thrashing about violently in the water.

"It's okay," she called as she reached out to him. "Just relax! Let me do all the work."

She had done this several times before, with people heavier than Thad. If he would just do as she told him, she'd have him safely on the beach in no time. If he was completely waterlogged, she'd call an ambulance. If he was okay, she'd call his parents.

Then she could go back to David.

She never even saw Thad's hands reach out for her. One minute, those hands were wildly searching the air for something to hold onto, the next minute they were fastened, viselike, around her neck. She couldn't breathe.

And he was dragging her down, down, into the blackness beneath the foamy waves.

Chapter 22

David had hurried along the beach some distance before he finally decided he'd been traveling in the wrong direction. The beach on this side of the clubhouse was totally deserted. He turned and, throwing off his tuxedo jacket and dropping it carelessly to the sand, began running back up the beach. Shannon, where *are* you, ran round and round inside his head. He knew absolutely nothing about the "old boyfriend." Was Shannon safe with him? Had she gone willingly with him? Or was there something really wrong and scary here?

When he ran past the clubhouse stairs, he wondered briefly if he should run up there and ask for help. Deciding he didn't want to waste more precious moments, he kept going.

Shannon had to be here somewhere. She *had* to!

The water closed over Shannon's head like a heavy woolen blanket. She saw nothing but blackness. Salty water filled her nose, her ears, the mouth she had opened instinctively when Thad closed off her windpipe. His fingers clung to her throat. Taken by surprise, her good judgment deserted her and panic took over, sending her limbs flailing about her wildly as she tried desperately to free herself.

A part of her detached itself then, thinking, So this is what drowning feels like. The pain in her chest from lack of air was unbearable. Her body felt incredibly heavy, as if weighted down by cement. Her head filled with a monstrous roaring sound. Had those people she'd rescued from the ocean felt like this? She had always thought it strange that even after they were safe on the beach they'd continued to shake with terror. She understood that now. They had been convinced they were dying, out there in the sea.

Not out *there*. Out *here*. Because she was, now, where they had been. And she was every bit as frightened.

Thad was willing to die, she was sure of that now. His thrashing about was simple instinct. But he would never have stepped into the ocean if he still cared about living. And if she didn't free herself, he'd take her down with him.

She stopped flailing. Panic would kill her faster than Thad's fingers stealing her precious air. She should have remembered that.

The buoyancy of the salt water bounced them back up to the surface. But the sweet air her lungs cried out for was denied her by Thad's grip.

B.J., she thought. Marilyn. Mom. I should have been a better sister, a better daughter. David.

No! She wasn't ready to give up. Not without a fight.

He dragged them down again, pulling on Shannon with his full weight.

She had to loosen his grip around her throat. Her strength was fading fast. Dizziness and disorientation would follow swiftly and she'd be lost among the dancing waves. So would Thad.

I can't drown, she thought with sudden clarity. I'm a *lifeguard*. I'd look like a total fool!

A mad desire to laugh at that ridiculous thought seized her. She fought it, afraid hysteria was setting in. That would be dangerous.

Do it *now*, Shannon, she ordered, while you still can. Gathering together every single ounce of strength she had left, she kicked as hard as she could to propel them upward. The second they broke the surface, she drew her weary left arm back as far as it would go, said a quick prayer, and propelled it as well as she could toward Thad's face.

With a sharp, satisfying crack, the arm connected with his chin.

Thad went limp.

And his fingers left her throat.

She grabbed his shirt collar, gripping it tightly even as she gulped in huge, delicious swallows of salty sea air. Careful not to hyperventilate, she concentrated on regulating her gasps, until the pain in her chest eased somewhat and all the tiny colored spots dancing before her eyes disappeared.

Never, never had air tasted and felt so wonderful. I will never smoke, Shannon vowed. I will never live in a polluted city. I will never again close the windows in my bedroom, even in the dead of winter. And I will never take anything as simple and ordinary as air for granted again.

She was alive.

Thank you, God.

Her throat throbbed with pain, her chest felt like a load of bricks had been dropped on it, and she had never been so tired in all of her life.

But she was alive. And so was Thad.

Now all she had to do was pray like crazy that he wouldn't come to until she had him on shore. How much power had her punch packed?

Well, she could always sock him a good one again. If she had to.

Her arm around his neck, she began stroking through the water, aiming straight for shore.

Poor Thad. Why hadn't she guessed how much trouble he was in? She should have talked to his parents. Why hadn't they noticed what was happening to him?

What it must have taken for him to wade into the shallows! He couldn't have known what he was doing. Or else he just hadn't cared.

Thad wasn't responsible for what he'd tried to do — he was sick. But what was *her* excuse for not doing anything about it? They could both have drowned, and it would have been her fault.

No, that wasn't right. How could it be her fault? She hadn't made Thad the way he was. His crush on her, obsession, whatever, may have made him worse, but he must have been shaky even before she'd met him, or all of this never would have happened.

The moon slid out from behind a cloud. She could see the shore now, faintly, just an outline. Had somebody moved it when she wasn't looking? It seemed awfully far away.

She was so tired. . . .

David was just about ready to give up and go inside to recruit fellow searchers when he thought he saw something moving in the water. Could be nothing more than a clump of seaweed. The "seaweed" moved. A pale arm sliced through the air. And the pale arm was dragging something along with it.

He could see no more than that, but that was enough. He turned back toward the noisy, lighted clubhouse. Two people, one tall, one short, had just come down the stairs.

"Call an ambulance!" he shouted. "Hurry!"

Lauren turned and ran back inside. Neal ran in the opposite direction, following David as he ran down toward the water.

Blaine was coming out of the rest room when Lauren raced past her to the wall telephone. She heard Lauren's frantic message to the operator. "Someone is in trouble in the water. Drifting Dunes Beach Club, Oceanview Road. Hurry!" Then Lauren hung up and ran back outside.

Blaine tried to tell herself that the phone call couldn't possibly have anything to do with Shannon or Thad or David. But she hadn't seen David come back into the clubhouse, with or without the Murphy girl.

She was already in trouble, both with Jeff and with David, and would be in more trouble with her parents the minute David told them how she'd tricked Shannon. But she could probably talk her way out of those things. No major crime there. But if someone drowned . . .

She'd better go see for herself what was happening on the beach.

She followed Lauren outside.

Shannon's arm around Thad's neck was cramping. She wanted desperately to let go, just for a second. But she knew she couldn't. She would lose him among the waves.

Buoyed by the salt water he hated, Thad weighed less than she'd feared. It amazed her that he hadn't even removed his jacket before he'd jumped into the water.

Maybe he had realized, there at the edge of the water, that he couldn't *make* someone love him. And then maybe he didn't care anymore what happened to him.

She hoped with all her tired, aching heart that someone would love Thad one day. When he was okay again. Because everyone needed that. Maybe Thad needed it more than most people. Or he wouldn't have done what he'd done.

She was almost there. Off to her right, the glow from the lights of the clubhouse came into view.

Faint strains of music reached her ears over the roar of the waves.

She was going to make it.

Lauren and Neal heard the distant wail of the ambulance as they ran along the beach. "I think that's Shannon in the water," she said, confusion in her voice. "What on earth . . . ?"

"Looks like she's got someone with her," Neal pointed out as they caught up with David. "What kind of fool would tackle the ocean at night?"

"No one in his right mind," Lauren said, completely unaware of just how accurate that comment was.

They ran together down into the shallows to help David pull Shannon and her burden onto the safety of the beach.

Chapter 23

Thad came to, just as Shannon was dragging him into the shallows. But he was too exhausted and disoriented to struggle. Shannon, every bone in her body aching, dragged him the last few feet and then collapsed beside him, her breath coming in short, ragged gasps. Shallow little rivulets of water pooled around them, teasing them gently, as if to say, You are safe now, but never play games with the ocean again. It is much more powerful than you.

"Shannon!"

David's voice. And in the background, rapidly coming closer, the eerie wail of a siren splitting the night air. Shannon was too tired to wonder who had summoned it so quickly.

"Shannon? Are you okay?"

And then strong arms were around her, clutching her to a very warm, dry chest. The arms held her and rocked her sodden, shivering body, whispering in her ear that someone was very glad she was safe.

She had made it back.

Other voices joined the one murmuring into her

ear. The voices belonged to . . . Lauren. And Neal. Expressing concern for her. People cared about her. She snuggled gratefully into the warm chest. She would simply stay there forever. Here, she wouldn't have to worry about anything.

Thad stirred and moaned, then began coughing violently. Lauren and Neal bent to pull him from the little rivers of water swirling around him, while David picked up Shannon and half carried her up the beach.

The ambulance screeched to a halt, splattering sand every which way with its tires. Shannon knelt by Thad's side and took one of his clammy hands in her own. "Thad," she said softly, looking down into his face. "Thad, it's okay. You're all right now. We're safe on the beach."

No answer. The coughing countinued for a few more seconds. Then Thad lay back quietly, his eyes closed.

"Thad, look at me! I know you're conscious."

The ambulance attendants arrived with a stretcher. "He need CPR?" one asked brusquely.

He thinks we're just a bunch of crazy kids who pulled a stupid stunt, Shannon thought. Well, what did it matter what he thought? It wasn't important. She shook her head. "I don't think so." She lifted her head, and her eyes met Blaine's. She had followed Lauren and Neal. And although it was perfectly clear to Shannon that whatever had happened here had been at least partially Blaine's responsibilty, Shannon saw not a shred of guilt in the girl's face.

"Blaine," she croaked through her aching throat, "I think you should be the one to call Thad's parents."

Her meaning was unmistakable. Blaine shifted uncomfortably on the sand.

"They're the only Wilcox in the phone book," Shannon continued in a flat voice. "Tell them to meet the ambulance at Oceanview Hospital. And hurry up!"

Blaine turned without a word and hurried back up the beach.

"Shannon, what happened to your throat?" Lauren asked, kneeling to get a better look.

Shannon waved a hand. "Nothing. It's okay." Bending toward Thad again, she whispered. "Thad, promise me you'll get some help."

His breathing was erratic, his eyes closed. But he said, so quietly that she had to almost lay across his chest to hear the words, "You should have let me die. Why didn't you let me die, Shannon?"

"Look, lady," one of the attendants said, "we've got a job to do here. Talk to him at the hospital, okay? And from the look of you, we need a second stretcher."

"No! I'm not going to the hospital. I'll be fine. And just give me a minute with him, will you? It's important!" She turned back to Thad. "That's stupid, Thad. Dying is stupid when you don't have to do it. Promise me right this very minute that you'll get help."

He rolled his head toward her then, and opened

his pale eyes. And he seemed to see her, her face white and strained, her red hair hanging in thick wet clumps around her face and shoulders, her dress dripping salt water and bits of seaweed.

"Why didn't you love me, Shannon?" he whispered. "That's all I wanted."

Lauren let out a soft "Oh," and Neal whistled through his teeth. Shannon's eyes filled with tears. David took one of her hands and held it in his.

"You didn't really love me, Thad," she said softly. "You just wanted me to belong to you. People can't belong to other people. If you'll get some help, you'll learn that for yourself."

He sighed then and turned his head away. "Okay," he said without emotion, "whatever you say. It doesn't matter."

Shannon sank back on her knees, leaning against David, still behind her, still holding her. Remembering their terrifying struggle in the water, Thad's fingers around her throat, she wanted to hate him. But she couldn't. She felt only pity for him. This sad, confused, half-drowned boy lying on the beach hadn't been able to handle things the way ordinary people did. He was drowning, she thought, long before he ever went near the water.

"It *will* matter," she said softly. "Just get better, okay?"

Then she let David help her to her feet, as the attendants took Thad away. She had refused to go, too, saying she was fine, just fine.

And she would be.

When the ambulance had disappeared into the darkness, Lauren spoke first. "What was that all about? Are you okay, Shannon?"

Shannon smiled weakly, her head against David's chest. "Could I tell you about it later? Why don't you guys go on back to the dance. And yes, I'm okay. Honest." She glanced toward the clubhouse. "I'm just glad the music was so loud that no one heard the ambulance. A crowd would have collected down here." She shuddered. "Who needed that?"

Reluctant to leave, but sensing that Shannon and David wanted to be alone, Lauren said she'd talk to them later, and led Neal away.

When they had gone, David lifted Shannon's chin to look into her eyes. His expression held a mixture of relief and concern. "Why didn't you tell me about that guy?"

"Could we sit, please?" She sank to the sand. Sadness overwhelmed her as powerfully and completely as Thad's grip on her throat had earlier. She had to tell David a story that would almost certainly turn him off completely. He'd know that dating Thad meant she didn't have enough sense to come in out of the rain. But she was too drained to keep secrets. Besides, she wanted to believe that he had a right to know. That would mean that they had a real relationship.

He put an arm around her and repeated his question.

She told him the whole story. "I couldn't tell you," she finished in a froglike croak. "At first, I didn't know you well enough. Then, when I did, I thought you'd think I was totally stupid for dating someone as screwed up as Thad. Like my own head must be as full of butterflies as his was." She glanced over at David. "Birds of a feather?"

"I would never have thought that, Shannon. And I'm not thinking it now. Look," he said, standing up and pulling her gently upright, "why don't we forget about this stuff for now? I invited you to a ball and it must be winding down by now. I don't want to be cheated out of that last dance. Let's go, okay?"

Shannon stared at him. "Are you crazy? Look at me!"

"I *am* looking. You're beautiful."

Shannon kicked him.

"Okay, so you can't go like that. Agreed. But that's no problem. Our cabana is just up the beach. You can freshen up there, as they say in the movies. You can even take a quick shower if you want, wash off the seaweed. But 'quick' is the operative word here, okay?"

"David. In case you haven't noticed, this dress would make a great Halloween costume right now."

He took her elbow and began leading her up the beach. "You can change at the cabana. If I know Blaine, you'll have more than one choice. There are probably at least half a dozen bikinis in there, to start with."

Shannon made a sound that was remarkably similar to a snort.

"Okay, okay, no bikinis. But we also keep a bunch of robes in there. Long ones, like to your toes. Take your pick."

A nice, warm robe sounded almost as wonderful as the prospect of a hot shower. Even a quick hot shower. But, "I'm not walking into the ballroom in a bathrobe, David."

They had reached the Hamilton cabana. He gave her a quick hug. "No need. The Dunes has terraces and decks all over the place. We can hear the music on any one of them just fine. But I *am* going to have that last dance. So get a move on. I'll wait right here." He planted a firm kiss on her salty lips. "Remember, the key word is 'quick.' Go ahead. Think slow dance. That'll get you moving."

The hot shower was so comforting, she had a hard time keeping the word "quick" in mind. Although Blaine had stocked the cabana with every kind of beauty aid, including a hair dryer and hot rollers, Shannon skipped all of that, towel-drying her hair briefly and letting the damp red curls hang loose. Then she enveloped herself in a thick, fluffy, white full-length terry robe and matching scuffs before joining David outside.

"You're gorgeous," he said as she left the cabana.

He put an arm around her shoulders and led her to the clubhouse. And on the way, he expressed sympathy for Thad. And never once joked about how she had driven someone crazy. Some boys would have, she knew. She was glad David wasn't one of them.

"But if anything like that ever happens to you again," he said as they climbed the stairs to the deck, "you come to me, okay? We'll work it out together. Promise?"

"I promise." What a nice word "together" was. What a lovely, wonderful word!

Still, she had saved Thad and herself on her own, and that felt good, too. Maybe "together" was just better when you weren't so desperate about it, the way Thad had been. When you knew you could handle things alone okay, but knew you didn't always have to. Was that what made the difference?

When they reached the deck, "Good Night, Ladies" was just beginning. Shannon knew it was a corny, old-fashioned song. She didn't care. This band played it very slowly, softly, and romantically. She loved it.

David smiled down at her. "May I have this dance?" He held out his arms.

She walked into them without a word. I will, she thought soberly, always, always remember those awful minutes out there in the darkness when Thad made the ocean my enemy. But when I do, I'll push those terrible thoughts away and think of this instead. I'll remember dancing this slow dance with David, his arms around me, my head on his chest, the smell of the ocean salty-sweet and not frightening at all. I'll feel his heart beating and I'll hear the music and I'll see the lights shining from inside the clubhouse. And I'll remember how calm and peaceful everything is now, how time slows down during a dance like this one and no one is in a hurry for anything else to happen. This is enough. I'll remember that.

She smiled and hummed the tune softly as they moved across the deck, her scuffs making little whispery sounds on the wooden floor.

Blaine, who had threatened Rick with no ride home in her Mercedes if he didn't dance this last dance with her, stomachache or no stomachache, saw David and Shannon through the long, narrow window. And she hated both of them. It wasn't fair. It just wasn't fair!

Jamie, her head on Alex's shoulder, saw David and Shannon, too. She had heard only vague rumors about some incident down on the beach, and she was happy to see that Shannon seemed okay.

And so am I, she thought. So am I.

And because she felt so okay, inspiration struck her and she lifted her head. "Alex," she said softly, "I would rather dance with you than with anyone else in the world. But would you be really upset if we traded partners with another couple?"

The nicest thing then was, he never even glanced in Jeff's direction. So he wasn't suspicious about that. And he must have known what she had in mind because he smiled and said, "Sure. Great idea! Just don't forget who you're going home with, okay?"

"Not in a million years." She reached up and touched his cheek with her hand. "Thanks, Alex."

They approached the dancing couple.

"Daddy," Jamie said, "may we cut in?"

Lauren, dancing with Neal past the window overlooking the deck, smiled with relief. Shannon was fine now, that was perfectly clear.

Time was standing still for Shannon and David just as it was for everyone else dancing this last, lovely slow dance.

And speaking of shallows, Lauren had, finally, made some good choices tonight, important ones, choices that made her feel good about herself. She bent her head and put it on Neal's shoulder.

Thousands of tiny clear lights in the ballroom twinkled as the band played on.

About the Author

DIANE HOH grew up in Warren, Pennsylvania, "a lovely small town on the Allegheny River." Since then, she has lived in New York State, Colorado, and North Carolina. Ten years ago, she and her family settled in Austin, Texas, where they plan to stay. "Reading and writing take up most of my life," says Ms. Hoh, "along with family, music, and gardening."

Slow Dance is Ms. Hoh's seventeenth book for Scholastic.